...ning and deeply true, it's a story about the red thread' that binds a family together through illness and change, and the love of a dog."
– Sinéad O'Hart, author of *The Eye of the North*

"A simply perfect book about a boy and his dog navigating a painfully well-observed imperfect situation... Funny and warm and ultimately leaves a glow."
– Perdita Cargill, author of *Waiting for Callback*

"Heartbreakingly brilliant! Warm, funny, sad, tender, with poetry that punches your heart."
– Tamsin Winter, author of *Being Miss Nobody*

"A gorgeous uplifting story about dogs, step-families and how they come in all shapes and sizes, and the difference a great teacher can make."
– Rhian Ivory, author of *The Boy Who Drew the Future*

"Warm, funny, kind, heartbreaking in places, but most of all just so vivid. It'll stay with me for ages!"
– Nicola Penfold, author of *Where the World Turns Wild*

"The story of a young boy who navigates his way through the tricky territory of family changes and new relationships with his beloved pet dog. A masterpiece in observation. Tender, humorous, important."
– Rachel Delahaye, author of *Mort the Meek*

"A truly lovely book. My heart is thoroughly warmed!"
– Sh   or   of *The H   f Hidden Wonders*

"A wonderful tale, told with heart, hope and a shiny wet nose".
– Gill Lewis, author of Swan Song

"A really special book".
– Hilary McKay, author of The Skylarks' War

"A story full of humanity".
– Cath Howe, author of Ella on the Outside

– Sharon Gosling, author of The House of Hidden Wonders

STRIPES PUBLISHING LIMITED
An imprint of the Little Tiger Group
1 Coda Studios, 189 Munster Road,
London SW6 6AW

Imported into the EEA by Penguin Random House Ireland,
Morrison Chambers, 32 Nassau Street, Dublin D02 YH68

www.littletiger.co.uk

First published in Great Britain by Stripes Publishing Limited in 2021
Text copyright © Ros Roberts, 2021
Illustrations copyright © Thy Bui, 2021

ISBN: 978-1-78895-320-7

Printed and bound in the UK.

The Forest Stewardship Council® (FSC®) is a global, not-for-profit organization dedicated to
the promotion of responsible forest management worldwide. FSC defines standards based
on agreed principles for responsible forest stewardship that are supported by environmental,
social, and economic stakeholders. To learn more, visit www.fsc.org

2 4 6 8 10 9 7 5 3 1

ROS ROBERTS

DIGGER

AND

ME

LiTTLE TiGER
LONDON

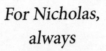

For Nicholas,
always

Monday 4th June

What do I *like*?

I can tell you what I *don't* like.

I don't like Philip's bogey. He's just wiped it on the back of his chair. It's stretched out, staring at me, green and squishy.

Mr Froggatt bounces past, tapping the tables.

"Who wants to start?" he says, spinning round. He leans over my desk and looks at the name on my English book. "James, yes?"

I nod and sit up a little.

"Well, James? What are some of the things you like?"

So I tell him.

Well, I tell him the version he wants to hear.

"My dog." That one's the truth, of course.

"Cool," he says. "Anything else?"

"Football," I say. Which I don't really. I play, of course. Because you kind of have to. Or need to.

"Do you like defending or attacking, James?"

Philip sniggers.

I'm not sure what to say. Uncle Bobby taught me how to play in goal and I always go there so I say, "Um, in goal, I suppose."

"OK. Goalkeepers are vitally important." He looks at the ceiling and taps his feet, jigs a little. He's thinking hard. "That's it! Guillermo Ochoa. Mexican goalkeeper in the 2014 World Cup. Outstanding!"

I nod as if I know what he's talking about. Uncle Bobby would have known.

"Look him up," says Mr Froggatt, and he spells out his last name O–c–h–o–a and I can see Tomaz writing it on the back of his hand.

Mr Froggatt makes a move as if he's saving a goal, diving across the room.

"Brilliant. Right, James, anything else?"

Wow, he wants more. So I think for a second.

"YouTube," I say. "Burgers, swimming … school."

He kind of jumps back and looks at me. "School? You like school? Well, that's amazing. I love that! Do you really?" He smiles as if I must be having a laugh.

Which I am, of course. No one likes school.

Philip turns round, his lip pulled, eyes narrow.

"As if," he says.

"And you, my friend?" says Mr Froggatt, moving to Philip's table. "You seem to be surprised." He leans to look at Philip's book. "Mr Davies, Philip Davies, what things do *you* like?"

Philip folds his arms. "Not much," he says.

"Gardening, peas," says Mr Froggatt. "Bearded dragons, making sandcastles, trampoline parks... There must be something. The world is full of things to like, Philip."

Philip shrugs. "I like killing things."

Mr Froggatt tilts his head and looks puzzled.

"On computer games," adds Philip.

"Well, that's a relief," says Mr Froggatt. "I had you out in the playground swatting flies, Philip, which would not be good. Even flies deserve to live." He twists his bow tie. I've never seen a teacher wear a bow tie. "What games do you play?"

Philip jerks up a little. This is fun, watching him squirm. "I play with my brother," says Philip. He sits back and flicks his hair the way he does when he's bothered. Then he slumps down and taps the desk with his pencil. "Just aliens and stuff, you know."

Mr Froggatt nods. "You've been honest, young man. A lot to be said for that."

Curveball.

Philip was honest. Philip told the truth.

Was I honest?

Not completely.

I stare out of the window at the school field and goalposts and I think of Uncle Bobby and my tummy aches a bit.

"Anyone else?" says Mr Froggatt.

India's hand goes up and we are now on very, very safe ground. You can feel it round the room. Go, India. He won't be able to stop India listing the things she likes.

"Yes?" says Mr Froggatt.

"I love dance, sir, and jewellery and my cat and my rabbit and seeing my grandparents and going to the beach and I *love* making sandcastles. And," says India, glancing round the room, "school and my friends and this great kit I've got at home for making wooden animals."

"Cool," he says. "Do you need tools to use the kit?"

India grabs a curl and twists it.

"I don't know," she says. "I haven't opened it yet."

"Well," says Mr Froggatt. "Let me know when you've found out."

India nods and smiles and says she will.

He asks us to open our exercise books. He wants us to write a poem about things we like. It can be any length, it can rhyme or not, it can be in any form.

"I'm going to write one too. Keep it simple if you want. Food, weather, TV shows. Just think of things that are important to you."

Tomaz makes a face like it's the last thing he wants to do.

Jack puts his hand up and says, "I don't do poems, sir."

Mr Froggatt moves to Jack's desk and looks at his book for his name.

"Well, tell me, Jack – what *do* you like to do?"

"Play football," says Jack.

"I'd like you to make a list," says Mr Froggatt. "Your ten favourite players and the five best games you've watched. Write them all over the page and make some of the letters link up. Like a piece of art."

"Really?" says Jack.

"Really," says Mr Froggatt. He has his own book, with his name on the front. He sits down at his desk with a pencil and starts to write.

I open the book and write 'What I like' on the top line.

I should start with Digger.

India's pencil steams across the lines. She's halfway down the page already. Flo asks for a word that rhymes with bear. Tomaz snaps his lead and then sharpens it over and over until it breaks again.

Philip flicks his pencil across the room. It rolls near Mr Froggatt's desk but Mr Froggatt keeps writing. Then he underlines something and stands up.

We all sit, very quietly, waiting to see what happens. He leans down and picks up the pencil. He walks over to

Philip's desk and puts it very gently on his page.

"Whoops," says Mr Froggatt, and then he walks back to his seat, sits down and picks up his book. "I think I'm nearly there," he says. "Anyone else?"

A few hands go up.

"Couple more minutes," says Mr Froggatt.

Tomaz and I share a look. He holds up his empty page. I show him mine.

And then I think about what I like and I start to write.

WHAT I LIKE

I like beans and sausages and my dog Digger
I like swimming and YouTube and American football
That's bigger
Than football
My dad went to America
Bought me a cap
Digger sits on my lap
I like my room
I like to sweep up leaves with the garden broom

Mr Froggatt stops us.

"Anyone want to share?"

"We haven't really done this before," says Margo.

"Good time to start," says Mr Froggatt. "But also, fine not to. Poetry can take you either way. Tell you what, I'll share mine. Is that OK?"

He waits for an answer. As if someone is going to say no.

"Have you really written one, Mr Froggatt?" asks Flo.

"Of course," he says. He stands up and walks in front of his desk. "I'll read it to you."

I like to teach
I like the beach
I like three sugars in my cup of tea
Crunchie bars
Moonlight and stars
Driving with a view of the sea
TV soaps
Climbing ropes
A steaming hot bubbly bath
Feeding my cat
A ball and bat
Making a stranger laugh

The bell rings out.

"It's funny," says Margo. "I like it."

"Well, that's my small offering," says Mr Froggatt. "Time for break." We jump to our feet. He claps his hands very loudly and we stop. "But chairs under, desks tidy." And then Mr Froggatt turns away, as if he doesn't have to check whether we will do it or not.

We push the chairs under and start filing out. India stops by Mr Froggatt's desk.

"What's your cat called?" she asks. We stop and listen.

"James Bond," says Mr Froggatt. "He's black and white, like James Bond in his suit."

"My cat's ginger," says India.

"I bet he's called Marmalade," says Mr Froggatt.

"No," says India. "He's called Ginger." She runs to catch up with Flo.

"Completely logical," says Mr Froggatt, to no one in particular.

"How is he?" says Mum.

"Who?"

"The new teacher."

"Oh." I cut my chicken into tiny pieces. "Yeah, nice.

Wacky."

"Wacky?" says Dave.

I shrug.

"What do you mean?" says Mum.

"He wears bow ties and jumps around and wants us to write about things we like."

"Oh, not one of those," says Dave.

"I like him," I say. Which is true. He's got Philip sussed. He saw the bogey and made him clean every chair in the room.

Digger scratches at the utility-room door. His big brown eyes stare through the glass. It's Dave's new thing. No Digger under the table while we eat. Dave found one golden hair in his roast beef and that was it. Digger was chucked out. It's not Digger's fault he moults. Digger has always been under the table. He was there before Dave knew what this table looked like.

"Well, let's just hope this one stays," says Mum.

She probably feels the same way about Dave. Let's hope this one stays, not like Russell, her last boyfriend, who didn't stay very long at all.

"How many teachers have you had now?" she asks.

"Three," I say.

"That school's got problems," says Dave. He sits back and scratches his bald head.

Dave has never set foot in my school.

"Three teachers in nine months isn't great," says Mum. "But it's not Mrs Jenkins's fault she had a baby. And Mr Bradshaw... Well, he's better with the infants really, isn't he, James?"

I shove a piece of chicken into my mouth. How should I know?

"Our Sean's school," says Dave, "was a flagship compared to this wreck. Turns out right clever kids."

Dave's son Sean is twenty-one. The only thing I've seen him do is drink beer. Which he does a lot. And the only clever thing I've seen him do is spin the beer bottle twice in the air, then catch it.

"Maybe we should look at moving him," says Dave.

I flick a loose pea off my plate. In the direction of Dave. Dave has lived here since Easter and he thinks he can *move* me. First Digger was moved to the utility room and now me. Shipped off to Sean's old school on the other side of town. I'd like to move Dave. I'd like to move Dave to another country and stick bogeys all over him. Dave could be a bogey sculpture.

People could buy tickets.

Bogey Dave, Bogey Dave, come and see him if you're brave...

I lean down and pick the pea up off the floor, forcing my smile to lie low. I line it up with the others, my little troop of pea rebels.

"There's only seven weeks left," says Mum. "Then he's off to high school." She lays her hand on Dave's arm. "Sweet of you to be concerned though."

"We could ask my cousin Clare too," says Dave. "They're looking at loads of schools right now for their little 'un."

Did you not hear, Dave? Seven weeks left? Think you might need your ears cleaning out.

"I think we're sorted, love," says Mum. "But we must have Clare and her family over soon. How old's Jake? Three?"

Dave nods.

"You'd like to meet Jake," says Mum, "wouldn't you, James?"

I can't imagine anything worse so I just say, "Can I get down?"

Mum looks at me and I can tell she's disappointed but she nods.

Dave sits back in his chair and sips his beer.

"Want to watch the footie?" he says to me. "Big game tonight."

"No thanks," I say. "I have homework."

"Wow, homework," says Mum. "I like it. What's the teacher called?"

"Mr Froggatt," I say.

"Great name," says Mum.

I go to fetch Digger. He stands up when he sees

19

me coming and his tail goes crazy. I take Digger by the collar and lead him to my room and give him the treat I saved in my pocket. He lies down on the rug and I lean on him and reach over to my bag and take out the homework. Mr Froggatt gave us all an envelope. One each, sealed.

"Find a quiet space," he had said as he handed them out. "And have a go."

I open it and pull out a postcard-sized piece of paper. There is a little note attached to it.

Hello!
Mr Froggatt here.
Can you draw me something in your home that makes you smile?
It doesn't have to be a drawing. It could be a photo or a collage.
Have fun! It will be great to see your ideas tomorrow!

I find a pencil from my bag and start to draw. I draw Digger with his long golden fur and his velvet ears and chocolate eyes. And then I need colours so I get my wooden box out. Uncle Bobby gave it to me the Christmas before he died. It has a pull-up section with two layers of pencil crayons. There are shades of every colour and they all have great names like loganberry and ultramarine. The card he wrote is still stuck to the inside of the lid.

Dear James,
Always see colour in the world.
And always go back to the future.
Love Uncle Bobby xxx

The card makes me smile. We used to play that game where you draw something and your team has to guess what it is. Me and Mum were on his team and he had to draw *Back to the Future*, which was one of his favourite films. He drew the mad professor's hair and Mum got it in a second and we won the game. We ran round the lounge screaming with joy, Digger darting from one person to the other, trying to work out what was going on. Dad and Gran didn't believe Mum had got it just from the spiky hair.

That was a long time ago and it's odd because Uncle Bobby was Dad's brother and Dad can't draw a thing.

I only need four colours. Goldy-yellow for Digger's fur, red for his collar and brown for his eyes. Choosing the fur colour is hard. I go for Aztec gold. And then I add a bit of black for his whiskers and his nose. When I'm done, I slide the drawing in the envelope and put it in my bag and I wonder what Mr Froggatt will do with our postcards.

Tuesday 5th June

"We've done this before," says Philip.

Mr Froggatt doesn't turn round from the whiteboard but speaks loudly. "You'll be an expert then, Philip." He draws lots of big, overlapping circles.

Philip snorts and mutters, "So boring."

Mr Froggatt stops. His pen hovers over the whiteboard. "That word is banned in my classroom," he says. He waits a second and then he starts drawing more big circles.

"Boring, boring, boring as…" says Philip. He says a very rude word.

Tomaz and I exchange a look. Here we go.

Mr Froggatt stops, turns round and sits on his desk. He is quiet for a minute. And then he walks to Philip's desk and gently lays down the whiteboard pen, right in front of Philip.

"The word 'boring' is banned from my classroom." He speaks quietly but firmly, making sure we all hear. "Would you like to teach the lesson on Venn diagrams?"

Philip turns his head away and looks out of the window.

Mr Froggatt picks up the pen, walks to the back of the room and sits down next to Jack.

We all wait.

Philip slumps lower in his seat.

A few minutes go by. And then a few more. Raj opens his book and reads. India starts plaiting her hair but then she drops the hairband and her chair scrapes and she giggles and I want to tell her to be quiet. Tomaz looks round at me and taps his watch. And then the bell goes. And still we wait. Until at last, Mr Froggatt gets up and tells us to go out to break.

The quiet follows us into the playground. Philip is up on the grass – it looks like he's digging. With his hands. Tomaz and I kick the ball but it's hot and my head aches so we just walk around, tapping the ball to each other.

"Want to come for a sleepover soon?" asks Tomaz.

"Course," I say.

"OK, I'll let you know when. We can play that new game I've got."

"Great."

He kicks the ball hard. It rolls up on to the field and we run after it.

When we come back in, the Venn diagrams on the

whiteboard have all been filled in. Mr Froggatt asks us questions about them. He asks Philip something quite simple and Philip gets it right and then Mr Froggatt moves straight on. It's like the thing that happened earlier is all forgotten. He knows that Margo understands absolutely everything about them but he asks her a really easy question and he asks Freya something really hard. Mr Froggatt has shaken it all up. Put everything in a blender like Mum uses, then poured it out in different bowls.

We do worksheets covered in Venn diagrams. There are hard ones and easy ones. We do them in groups. We help each other. Then Mr Froggatt gives us blank diagrams to fill in with our own topics. Me and Tomaz and Jack do a big one on Liverpool and Man City players. Jack knows everything about football. But even Jack can't think of a player to go in the middle bit.

"What's this?" says Mr Froggatt. He groans and looks at our sheet. "Very disappointing. And I was just starting to like you lot."

We don't know what to say. Tomaz bites his lip and Jack stares hard at the sheet, trying to work out where we went wrong.

Mr Froggatt shakes his head.

"Could you not have chosen a decent team, lads? United is the *only* team!" He points at each of us and smiles and we all laugh. "Good Venn diagram though," he says and he walks away, shaking his head. "Sterling and Milner," he calls back. "There's two for the middle."

"Course," says Jack and he writes Sterling in the middle bit. He spells it with a 'u' instead of an 'e' but I don't say anything.

Mr Froggatt asks us to push the desks to the edges of the room and he brings in a pile of hoops that we use in PE. We make giant Venn diagrams on the floor and he gives us cards to fill them.

When the bell goes for lunch, we move the desks back. Mr Froggatt asks to speak to Philip. I'm right there, beside Philip, so I hear him.

"Wash your hands before lunch," he says, very quietly. "You have a lot of mud on them. There's plenty of soap." He nods to the sink at the back of the room. Philip wipes his hands on his trousers and walks to the door. But Mr Froggatt is there before him and shuts the door firmly. Everyone is putting desks back, sliding chairs under, chatting and fetching jumpers. It's only me that's noticed, like I'm the referee.

Philip picks the mud from under his fingernails and lets it fall to the floor.

Mr Froggatt leans on the door, his arms folded.

"How's Ginger?" he asks India.

"She caught a shrew," says India. "Her first one."

Mr Froggatt mutters Philip's name and when he looks up, Mr Froggatt lifts his hands and shakes his head a little as if this situation is not going to change. It's like Dad last week when I left sweet wrappers on the car seat and he wouldn't open the front door until I'd fetched them. He's fussy about his cars, my dad. I just went straight back for the wrappers but Philip's not like me. He folds his arms and scrapes his shoes on the floor.

"Are you sure Ginger caught it?" asks Mr Froggatt. "Maybe she ordered it from Shrews R Us." India stares at him, trying to understand. "You know," he says, "next-day delivery, on the patio by six a.m."

I smile.

India nods and smiles too, but I can tell she hasn't got it.

Tomaz and Jack are staring out at the field. The Year 5s have claimed the best part.

"I'll be late for drama club," says Flo.

"Nearly there," says Mr Froggatt. "Just waiting for the last job to be done."

A few people check their chairs are under, desks are neat.

The noise in the corridor gathers.

Jack starts to get annoyed. Jack isn't much fun when he gets annoyed.

Finally, Philip walks to the sink and washes his hands,

pumping the soap dispenser until the soap drips through his fingers on to the paper towels stacked underneath.

Mr Froggatt opens the door and we file out.

"Next-day delivery gets you a bigger shrew," he says as we leave. He pats me on the shoulder. "Or a free vole."

After lunch, Mr Froggatt asks us to get our envelopes out.

"I forgot," says Jack.

"No worries," says Mr Froggatt. "I forget lots of things. Forgetful Froggatt, they call me."

We go to our bags and most of us come back with an envelope. India has a large box, covered in a black bin bag.

"It's my room," she says. She takes off the bag and shows Mr Froggatt. It's a shoebox painted purple with a cardboard bed, furniture, curtains and even a real piece of carpet on the floor.

"Astounding," says Mr Froggatt.

Tomaz stares at India's creation and holds up his piece of paper to show me. He's drawn a square with three small circles.

"The TV!" he whispers. "Took me five seconds." We both laugh.

"I've put a little washing line up, by the window," says Mr Froggatt. "You can either hang your picture on the line or lay it underneath to share and then take it home tonight. Your choice."

Most of us peg up the pictures. Jack has done a football. Raj has drawn his garden. Margo has made hers of Lego bricks in the shape of a spaceship. Freya has taken a photo of her snake. I choose the end peg and put Digger up, but then I'm not sure I've drawn his legs quite right. They look too small for his body. So I take him down and lay him underneath on the red display cloth.

Philip is hovering beside me. He takes a peg down but then he just folds his sheet and leaves it next to mine and walks away, clamping the peg on to his finger. Mr Froggatt watches him and then he opens Philip's drawing and looks at it carefully. I peer to see. It's a guitar. He has every detail. Uncle Bobby would be impressed. Philip has always been good at art. And then everyone laughs because India tries to peg up her room and the whole line droops.

"Let's put this here," says Mr Froggatt and he lays the box on a pile of textbooks to give it height.

"Sorry," says India. "I don't think I got it right."

"India," says Mr Froggatt. "I think it's brilliant! Just one problem."

India chews her nail and says, "It's too big."

"Nope," says Mr Froggatt. "I can't see Ginger."

"Oh, he's right there!" says India and she points to a tiny, curled-up shape, drawn on the end of the bed.

"Well, that's top marks for sure," says Mr Froggatt and then he points to Tomaz's picture of his TV. "And so is that! Reminds me of Picasso's line drawings." He walks away and Tomaz looks at me and polishes his fingernails on his jumper as if he is a genius.

Tomaz's mum picks us up after school. She drives a little blue car. We are going swimming. Tomaz has joined my swimming lessons and now our mums share the lifts. Mum doesn't do many trips. She often works late on a Tuesday. But that's OK because Tomaz's mum *always* has nice things to eat. She passes back a Tupperware full of food and two drink cartons.

"How was your day?" she says. She has a very strong Polish accent. I like listening to her. Sometimes she speaks to Tomaz in Polish and he answers her and it's like I don't know Tomaz. And then he speaks to me and he's just Tomaz again. I wish I could do that. I think it must be the most amazing thing in the world. Like being a secret agent.

They speak in Polish for a bit. I look out of the window and think about being a secret agent on a mission to save the world. We pass the pub we used to go to for Sunday lunch. Dad always moaned that the meat was tough but I liked it because it has a garden in the back with play stuff and a giant red dinosaur. I always check the dinosaur when we drive past. There are bad words written down the side. No one ever cleans them off. I suppose it would be hard to reach them but then I wonder how they got there. Maybe that's my mission, to swing up the dino's neck and wipe away the bad words, only to find a coded message underneath. The message would open the dino's neck and I would slip into a world of hidden passages and muddy caverns with a pile of hi-tech gadgets.

"What do you think?" says Tomaz.

I turn to face him.

"Sorry?" I say.

"About coming for the sleepover in a few weeks. Mum says the twenty-third of June would be good. It's our next free Saturday."

"Yeah, great," I say. I look back for the dino but we are past it now.

"I think just you two this time," says Tomaz's mum. She glances at us in the mirror. I catch her eye. I'm pleased. "That boy with the hair. I like him. Is it Mack? But I think he slept not at all, did he, Tomaz?"

"The boy with the hair?" says Tomaz and he looks at me and we both burst out laughing. Jack has this really cool razor fade. His dad's a hairdresser so he has it done all the time to keep it 'sharp' as Jack calls it. "You mean Jack," says Tomaz to his mum.

"Yes, Jack," she says. "Jack didn't sleep."

We turn in to the pool car park. I'm so ready to swim. All thoughts kind of go when I hit the water. I don't think Tomaz feels the same.

"It was so hard last week," he says, gripping his bag and staring at the big orange doors.

"No nervousness," says his mum. "Come on. James will help you if you have to do that bitterby thing."

"Butterfly, Mum," says Tomaz. "But James can do it really easily. I can't."

"Your backstroke is way better than mine," I say.

"Not really," he says, opening the car door. And it's true. It's not. Our backstroke is about the same.

It's odd with swimming now. Tomaz is my best mate but I liked it when I didn't know anyone. I loved jumping in, pacing up and down the lengths, looking up for the next set of tasks. It's different now because I have to stop and help Tomaz.

I told Mum and she said, "That's friendship. You have to give and take. Like me and Gena."

Gena is loud and bossy and talks so much it makes your head ache.

Tomaz is nothing at all like Gena.

31

Wednesday 6th June

"OK, so I'm super excited about this," says Mr Froggatt. He puts a small blue book down in front of each of us. "Write your names on the front."

I do it extra neatly. A new book in June is quite the thing. I wonder how Mr Froggatt has managed it.

"What's it for?" asks Raj.

"It's for you to find out when you take it home and have a go. You have very little time left in Year Six. High school is round the corner. But I want you to enjoy the last few weeks. I'd love you to try something new. It may help to prepare for high school."

"High school sucks," says Jack.

Philip gives a snort of approval.

India chews her nails.

"No, it doesn't," says Freya. "My sister loves high school. She gets to make things out of metal."

"I'm glad," says Mr Froggatt.

I sneak a look at the first page. If this book can help me grow like thirty centimetres of height, then I'm up for it. That's what I need to prepare for high school.

Tomaz is staring at the floor, head on his arms.

"I know it's a big change," says Mr Froggatt. "But often things will be what you make of them."

"Are you going to stay, sir?" asks Jack.

"What do you mean, Jack?"

"Well, are you just here for a week, like the supply teachers we had after Mr Bradshaw?"

Mr Froggatt sits on his desk at the front. "Look at me, all of you," he says and he claps his hands. I nudge Tomaz and he lifts his head. "I am going nowhere. You're stuck with me. From now to the end of term I am here for everything. Good and bad. Unless aliens come down from outer space and abduct me, I'm not going anywhere. You put bogeys on chairs, I'll know about it. You tease someone, I'll know about it. You want to talk, or cry, or laugh, I'm here."

We're all quiet. It's a bit like one of those scenes in the movies when the good guys are getting ready to move out, take on the mission. It's like Mr Froggatt really likes us. Us. Year 6. The class that scared Mr Bradshaw back to the infants.

"My name – Froggatt. It's an ancient name. I've looked it up. Part of it means I might look like a frog." Everyone laughs a bit. "Or my family might have lived near frogs. But it also means a home or shelter. Think of me as a little, froggy home."

The bell rings.

"Take the book home tonight. Read the first page. After that, it's up to you. Do it or don't. Give it in to me or don't. I'll be your froggy home either way."

"I've already started, sir," says India. She is scribbling away.

Tomaz and I stuff our things in our bags and head towards the door.

Philip is reading the first page. "As if," he says. He tosses the book on to the shelf but it catches a pot of pens and they fall.

Mr Froggatt puts the pens back and picks up Philip's blue book. He walks over to the window and watches Philip. He is outside already, running across the playground towards the school gates, his laces flapping around his ankles.

I walk home on my own some days but Mum is always there on a Wednesday; she gets an early shift at the dentist. She brings treats and she always brings Digger. I think it's because I go to Dad's house on a Wednesday evening so

Mum likes to squeeze in every bit of time with me she can.

"You OK?" she says. She passes me a biscuit.

"Yep." I bury my head in Digger's neck and tickle his side. His tail wags so hard that the people behind us have to wait to pass.

"Good day?" She pulls Digger gently and we set off.

"Yep."

"Headache gone?"

"Yep."

"Sure?"

I know what's she's doing. She wants me to say I don't feel well so I can stay at home tonight and not go to Dad's. We walk on in silence until we reach the grassy patch on the corner. Digger stops and turns in circles, arching his back.

"Oh, not here, Digger," says Mum, but we have no choice but to wait while he goes. Mum rummages for a bag to pick it up. She ties the handles and walks over to put it in the bin, then we set off again.

"Do tell your dad not to feed him raw meat again. His tummy was horrendous last time." I don't say anything. We turn the corner and walk down the long street to our house. "It would be much easier to just leave him at home."

"Digger is Dad's dog too," I say. "His home is with me. We agreed that right at the start."

When we get in, I have a drink and watch a bit of TV.

I pack a few things in my bag and then I grab Digger's kibble and fold his bed into a large black bin bag. The bed's a bit muddy. Kathy always has a right moan about the dirt and the hair. She moans about everything.

Digger sniffs at the bag of kibble, his tail wagging.

"Why don't you just leave him here?" says Mum. She opens the bag and gives him one piece and then seals it back up tight.

I stare at her hard.

"OK, all right," she says. "I get it."

The doorbell rings. Digger lifts his head. It rings over and over in sharp spurts. Sean. Dave lets him in but they don't say hi. They just do this thing where they lift their heads in a back-to-front nod. Digger is excited. He's always excited when someone comes. Even Sean. But Sean ignores him and goes straight to the garden to have a cigarette.

Mum's stroking Digger, pulling out loose hair. He has his head nestled against her. "There, that's better, my love," she says and she hugs him as if she won't see him again for weeks. "Why don't I just speak to your dad about Kathy and the hoovering episode?"

"No," I say. "It's sorted."

I made a huge mistake last week. I came home on Sunday and moaned about Kathy. I never moan about Kathy. I could. I could moan about Kathy all day. But I don't. Except last week Kathy had been in a bad mood and she was hoovering (she hoovers a lot) and she bashed Digger's paw. She didn't mean to. I know that. But Digger hid behind the sofa and we had to get fresh chicken to tempt him out. Kathy was actually quite worried and even turned the hoover off to check he was OK. When I told Mum, she wanted to know every last detail. I've never seen Mum so interested to hear *anything*.

The oven timer beeps. Mum's made beef casserole. It smells amazing.

"Sure you don't want a quick bite? Before you go."

I'm so tempted to have a bowl but I say no. "I'll eat with Dad, you know I will." It will be a takeaway. Or oven pizza. Or beans on toast.

Sean comes back inside. Dave gets two beers and passes one to him. Sean does the double-spin thing and they clink bottles. And then they flick off the tops and Sean tips his bottle back and gulps. It dribbles down his chin and he wipes it with his sleeve and then burps. Loudly.

A car horn beeps outside.

I grab the overnight bag and Digger's bed and put them by the front door and then go back for Digger. Mum is clipping on his lead.

"Come on, lad," she says. She snuggles into his neck. She hates it when Digger goes. She hates it when I go too but

I think it makes things a little easier for her. Gives her a chance to concentrate on Dave and Sean. One in, one out. And if Sean is here, I don't want to be.

I pull on the lead. Sean sniggers a bit because Digger won't move.

"Come on," I say.

Digger lifts one paw and scrapes it against me. I rub it. He likes that. It comforts him. Always has.

"Come on," I say. "Dad's outside."

Dave puts his beer down and ruffles Digger on the crown of his head.

"You'll be back tomorrow," says Dave, and he tickles him under the chin.

I pull the lead but he still won't budge.

"Footie's on," says Sean. "We're gonna miss the start."

He comes up behind and nudges Digger quite firmly with his foot. I start. But Dave is there before me.

"Don't," he says, and he stares at Sean.

Sean tips the beer bottle back, his eyes not leaving his dad's. Then he walks to the table and breaks off a piece of bread.

Dave and I share a little look. I want to say thanks but then that's the last thing I want to say because I would *never* say that to Dave. The look only lasts a few seconds. I don't think we've ever shared a look before. His eyes are a bit wrinkled and his eyebrows kind of droop, like they need to be trimmed. Which is odd as his head is bald. We shuffle round each other, me and Dave. Move in and out of the same space, like two sides of a Venn diagram. With Mum in the middle.

"Have a nice evening," says Mum. She hugs me.

I pull firmly on Digger's lead and he follows me out into the hall. My school rucksack is there. I grab the new blue book and shove it in the overnight bag and pick everything up. It's hard to walk with the bags and Digger but I'm used to it now. Mum doesn't come out with me when Dad's there. I slam the door shut.

Dad is leaning on the car. I can hardly hold Digger. He gets crazy excited when he sees Dad.

"Hey, James, watch out – I'm delivering this car tomorrow. Just had it cleaned." He moves forwards and takes Digger and they play-fight for a bit, like they always do. The car is bright red with spoilers. Dad hasn't had it long. It must have sold dead fast. It's cool how Dad sells cars. You never know what he's going to turn up in. He pulls me in for a hug.

"You all right, mate?" he says. "Everything OK? You banged that door good and hard." He stares at the house. I always want to know what he's thinking when he does that. He lived in that house for ten years. But I never ask.

Dad opens the boot and Digger jumps in. There is a huge blanket covering the floor and the back of the seats.

"There's a metal loop, just there," says Dad and we attach Digger's lead.

I'd love Dad to meet me on his own. But Kathy is always sat in the front passenger seat, and she always sniffs when she sees Digger, her nose angled away as if to stop the dog germs drifting up her precious nostrils.

I get in the back.

"You all right?" says Kathy.

I don't answer. I don't even nod.

The minute Dad sits down, Kathy leans over and picks hairs from his trousers.

"Just washed those, babe," she says.

"Does it matter?" he says.

She whips her hand away and stares out of the window, her arms folded.

I put my hand over the back of the seat to pat Digger. He places his head in my palm.

Kathy has cooked. She hardly ever cooks.

"Is it good, babe?" she says, stroking Dad's hair. His foot is linked with hers under the table. I can see through the glass surface. I hate this table. Everything scrapes on it. Digger never goes under this table.

"Lovely," says Dad. He's picked out the mushrooms. They are nestled in little bundles, struggling to stay hidden. He should line them up. Like my peas.

"What have they done wrong?" she says.

Uh-oh. They've been spotted. Dad keeps eating. He glances at my plate as if to check I haven't risked something so dangerous.

"Babe," says Kathy. "I thought you liked mushrooms?"

"You don't have to know absolutely *everything* about me," says Dad. "I don't like anchovies either." He pops a piece of chicken in his mouth and then he pours wine in her glass and leans towards her and whispers, "But you do know lots of things I like."

I want to vomit. I leave my pile of food in a little heap.

"I don't feel great," I say. "And I've got homework. Can I get down?"

"Course, mate," says Dad.

Kathy doesn't argue. She has her whole leg twisted round Dad's now. Yuck, yuck, yuck.

I get Digger from the front hall.

"Just one thing, James," says Kathy. She stops, as if she expects my attention. I stare at the door. Make a sound in my head to try and blank her out. "Please don't let Digger climb on your bed. There was hair everywhere last time."

I go to my room and sit on the floor and nestle into Digger. He lies down next to me and rests his head on my leg and I stroke his fur, over and over, letting the loose hairs drop on to the rug.

I open the new blue book on the first page.

Hello!
Good old Mr Froggatt here.
A poem to work on
Doesn't have to rhyme
I'll give you a theme
Just have a good time!
I'm not going to score it
With crosses and ticks
It's your own special work
There'll be nothing to fix
Write it, rhyme it,
Give haiku a go
I'll enjoy it whatever
So let the words flow.

Digger shifts a little and stretches out on the rug. I turn to the next page.

MY HOME
Describe your house,
big as a castle, small as a mouse.
(A house cannot really be as small as a mouse
unless you're a woodlouse!)

I start to write.

MY HOME

It has a red front door
With a welcome sign
To cover the crack.
When you open the door
My dog is there.
Right there
By the stair
And he don't budge
So you step over him and ruffle his hair.

His name's Digger
And if you tickle his back
His right leg goes mad with a scratch.
Philip did it for ages
So I told him he had to stop
But he wouldn't stop
So I told him he had to go
But he wouldn't go
So I tickled Philip's back
Quite hard
Then he went.
Digger only likes it a little bit.
There are hooks by the front door
One two three four
Mum, Dave and me
And one for Digger's lead.
Last night someone knocked on the door.
Mum said to open it.
The man said give this to your dad
I said which one?
He said the one you live with
I said he's not my dad
Oh he said.
I said he's what they call a stepdad
Right he said

Right what? I said

No, just right, I understand he said.

But I don't think he did.

Cos Dave's my sort of second stepdad.

I'm like a ladder

I've got lots of steps.

They all crack after a while and my mum slips off.

Like the ladder's made of ice

Like it melts when life stops being nice

And she slips

Right off

Right.

My house has a lounge and a kitchen and a little back bit,

The porch,

With my bike

Which I like

But I haven't ridden in ages.

Upstairs there are three rooms.

Mum and Dave in one,

Me in two

Dave's boxes in three.

My room has blue walls and rocket curtains.

Mum wanted to change them, she bought new

ones with footballs.

I said no.

Dad put the rockets up.
The rockets were here before Dave.
Years before Dave.
They were up before Dave and his shaggy eyebrows arrived.
My real dad doesn't live here, like I told the man at the door.
He lives miles away, my dad.
It's real bad.
I'm his lad.
It makes me mad.
As mad as a rocket.
I like my house.
There is a fruit tree in the garden
With stones in the winter
And fruit in the summer
And branches that fork and grow
And leaves that flutter, high and low.

I close the book. Digger lifts his head. So I open it again and read the poem to him, very quietly. He rests back down. When I'm finished, I stroke his golden head over and over. There is a sort of dome bit there, which I love, and it shines when you really smooth the fur.

"You're my home, Digger," I say. He stands up as if he thinks we are going to play. So I get up and lie on the bed and he jumps up with me. He's a bit big for this now but we've always played on the bed, ever since he was a puppy.

There's a knock on the door.

"You all right, mate?" It's Dad. "Can I come in?"

I don't answer. The door opens slowly and Dad comes in and shuts it behind him.

"What you doing on there?" he says, staring at Digger, but his voice is quiet and gentle. Dad sits on the edge of the bed, his legs stretched out in front of him. I grab the blue book quickly and tuck it under the duvet, out of sight.

"Everything OK?" he says.

I nod and cuddle into Digger.

"Your mum all right?"

I don't answer.

"You going to come downstairs and watch some TV with us?"

I shrug.

I'm irritated about my bike. I hadn't really thought about it before the poem.

"Can we ride our bikes soon?" I ask.

"Our bikes..." says Dad. "Wow, that's been a while,

eh?" He slouches next to me and ruffles my hair. "You're probably faster than me now."

"Doubt it," I say.

"And I bet you're too big for your old red bike?" asks Dad.

I shrug again. As if I know. It's hardly like I've grown much.

"I'm sure we can work something out."

Kathy walks in. No knock. Just comes in, tea towel over her shoulder. She is really dragging out this making dinner thing.

"Work what out, babe?"

"Oh, hi, love," says Dad. He sits up, as if slouching is a crime. "We were just talking about riding our bikes again."

"Oh," says Kathy. She pulls the tea towel down and twists the corner, tight. "You two did that back in the good old days, hey?"

Dad stares at her. He stands up and Digger jumps off the bed, nestles into Dad's leg.

The bed is a crunched-up doggy mess.

Kathy is pretending not to look, forcing her eyes away from the hairs and the crumpled duvet. She shakes out the tea towel and then folds it back up, over and over.

"Perhaps we could buy new bikes," says Dad. "One each. Make it a family trip."

Kathy nods. She smiles. Dad has said the right thing.

But he hasn't for me. We aren't a family.

"I like my old bike," I say. I slide off the bed and hook Digger's lead to his collar. "I don't want a new one." I leave the room, pulling Digger with me. The lead gets tangled. I unravel it and we dash downstairs and out of the front door, the letter box rattling as I slam the door hard.

Thursday 7th June

Thursday mornings are tricky. We have to drop Digger home before going to school and we are always running late. Dad is dusting the inside of the car for the tenth time.

"Needs to look as good as new," he says, which is odd because I thought the car was new. "We had fun, love, yeah?"

I want to say no. I don't think I ever have fun with Kathy. But I can't do that to Dad, so I say, "Yeah, of course."

"And we'll get some bikes soon."

I nod. "Three bikes will cost a fair bit," I say.

"Don't you worry about that, James," says Dad. "I've sold a lot of cars this month. Things are good."

When we arrive, Dave is loading his van. He has his overalls on, one strap hanging loose. Dad pulls up right behind him. I think he wants Dave to see the car.

Dave raises one hand in a wave.

"What does he do again?" says Dad, turning off the engine and lifting just a few fingers off the steering wheel to say hi to Dave. I don't know why he's asking. I'm sure he knows.

"He's a plumber," I say. "And a heating engineer."

"Blimey, he looks the part."

I don't like the way he sniggers.

"What do you mean?" I say.

"Well, he's got the van *and* the overalls. The whole shebang."

I pretend to laugh a bit because I think that's what Dad wants me to do. But I don't like it. Which is odd. Because I don't like Dave.

I jump out and grab my bag and Digger's bed and get him from the boot.

"You all right, mate?" says Dave, looking at me. I nod. Dave looks at his watch. "It's late. Shall I take Digger in?"

I pretend not to hear and walk up the path.

Mum opens the door. I dump the bag and the bed and pass her the lead. Digger is going mad, twisting around Mum's legs.

"Hey, love," says Mum. "How's things?"

"Fine," I say. She wraps her arm around me.

"Everything OK this time?"

"What do you mean?" I say and then I realize she's talking about the hoovering thing again. "Great," I say. "All great." I quickly hug Digger, grab my school bag and run back down the path and jump in the car.

Dad pulls off. He flicks the radio on and fiddles with the buttons. I think he's checking that it all works OK. When we get to school, he gives me a hug. I don't like his smell – he has new aftershave. It smells of the spray you use in the bathroom when you've done a really bad one.

Mr Froggatt has a box on his desk. It has a slit in the top and a big sign on the front:

POETRY BOOKS
Friday – Sharing Day

India is standing next to the box, reading through her poem. There are borders all around it, coloured-in swirls and decorations.

"Remember," says Mr Froggatt, "these are just between me and you, unless you want to share it with the class. Put a little note on it if you do."

India stops, just as she's about to slip her book down into the slot. She borrows a pencil from Mr Froggatt's desk and opens her book and scribbles something. She will share. India always shares.

I get mine out of my bag.

"You've done one?" says Tomaz. I nod and pop my book in the slot. "So have I," he says and he pulls his out and shows me.

My house is big
As big as a pig
But it is not pink
And the cat litter stinks.

"Cool," I say.

Mr Froggatt has laid out our maths books in a big fan. I find mine and wince. How has any human being *ever* understood long division?

"The work was varied," says Mr Froggatt. "But that's not a surprise. Long division was invented by someone who wanted the entire population of the world to get an enormous headache. Philip, don't scratch the desk. Do that again and I'll keep you in all of break, and all of lunch, sharpening pencils. Clear?"

Philip ignores him. Traces his pencil over the scratch mark.

"Is that clear?" says Mr Froggatt.

Philip says nothing but he puts down the pencil.

We begin our corrections. I look around the room. Margo has started a new sheet of problems, slipped inside her book. Margo has a brain the size of a pineapple.

Mr Froggatt helps us, moving from table to table. And then he sits next to Philip, very quietly, and helps him. He writes out the sums. He doesn't talk. Just writes them on the paper and shows Philip how to work them out. And then he pats him on the back and tells him he has done well. When Mr Froggatt goes back to his desk I look over and Philip is rubbing at the scratch on the desk, as if he is trying to make it disappear.

Mum is at the school gate, Digger on the lead.

"Good day?" she asks.

"Fine."

We set off down the road. Philip cycles past, his front wheel lifted. Tomaz waves from his dad's van.

"I'm glad you had a good time last night," Mum says. I don't answer. "I missed you," she adds.

I nod a little and make a sound that tells her I know.

We get caught behind a long line of parents and little kids. We turn the corner and speed up. Our house is ahead.

I can see Dave's van. He is there, opening the boot, lifting out something heavy.

"Oh, good," says Mum. "He remembered."

It's Digger's food. It comes in a big white bag. Dave puts it down on the pavement and closes the boot. Digger speeds up. He must have seen a cat. Or smelled something good in the hedge. I jog behind him. But Digger doesn't stop by the bushes. He keeps running, excited. And then I realize. He's seen Dave. He is pulling to get to Dave. And when we get there, he wags his tail like mad and Dave pats his head.

"Good day, mate?" he says, looking at me.

I want to say, *I'm not your mate*. But I can't. I want to say, *Thanks for getting the food*. But I can't. So I just walk up the path, tugging Digger behind me. I get to the front door and wait for Mum to unlock it. I can see her and Dave reflected in the glass. Dave is dragging the bag along the ground. It must have been the food. That's what Digger saw. The food. He pulled for his dinner.

Mum opens the door.

"Pizza for tea?" she says.

I nod and go inside and dump my bag and take Digger into the utility room and refill his water and clean his food bowl. I do it all very loudly. Digger is sitting, staring at me. He's not sure what's wrong. I'm not sure what's wrong. And then I get out his brush and I sit with him on the cool, tiled floor. I brush his golden fur over and over, until his coat gleams and the brush is full of hair. Mum slides the bag of food in beside me and passes me a drink. I brush Digger again, under the leg, and then I stop. I put the brush down and run my hands over the inside of his front leg. There is a lump. It's firm and round and it sticks out of his fur. I call Mum and she comes back in.

We make Digger roll. We make him sit so we can get a good look. We pull the fur back and we both feel the lump. Mum is a little quiet. She calls for Dave. He comes in, cup of tea in hand, and kneels down and he feels it too.

"Think we'll get that checked out," says Dave, laying his arm on Mum's back. And for the first time I don't mind that Dave has used the word 'we'.

The vet can't see Digger until tomorrow. We eat our pizza in silence, nibbling.

"It might be an infection," says Dave. "You know, he's caught himself on some wire and it's gone a bit nasty. Or it could be a fatty lump. Dogs get fatty lumps, just like we do. I've got some." He pulls up his sleeve and shows us. I move to look a little closer, hoping it looks just the same as Digger's lump. It doesn't.

"What if it's something else?" I say.

I want Dave to keep talking, to keep suggesting things that don't matter.

"Uncle Bobby had that lump," I say, "and that was the start of it all."

Mum reaches out and holds my hand. "Let's not think like that," she says. "Look at him. He's so fit and healthy."

We all turn to look at Digger. He is staring at us through the utility-room door, his breath making a little patch of mist on the glass. It's like he knows we are talking about him.

"He never had lumps when he was allowed under the table," I say. I can't help it. "He never had lumps then. When he wasn't shoved out all the time."

"That's not fair, James," says Mum.

"I literally don't care," I say. I push my plate away and get down and fetch Digger. He bounds up to me, grabbing a shoe to carry in his mouth. I lead him by the collar.

"James," says Mum, standing up as I pass. She moves to block my way. "Stop right there." Her tone is different. I stop. "This is important, James. Listen to me. Don't be upset and cross around Digger. He will pick up on it. Dogs sense things. He just needs to feel happy and loved."

I stare at her. I stare at her and then I look at Dave and back at her again.

"Exactly," I say. "Just like he used to. Like *I* used to."

And then I walk out. My words sting and float in the air, like burnt toast. I go to my room. I close the door. And then I lie down with Digger and I cry, very quietly, into his fur, trying my hardest, my very hardest, not to let Digger know.

Friday 8th June

The bell will go soon. I stare at the clock, wishing the minutes away. I just want to be with Digger. I just want to find out that he's OK. The lump seemed bigger this morning. Mum said it wasn't but I'm sure it was.

"'My home', by Raj," says Mr Froggatt. He looks round for Raj and starts to read.

It is small and warm and dry
I only leave it when I fly
My home is great, my home is the best
Twigs and feathers make up my nest.

"Great stuff," he says. "I like the way you made it about a bird."

He reads out India's poem next, which goes on and on, and then Eva's, which rhymes so well I'm relieved I didn't share mine.

"Did you do one, sir?" asks Margo.

He nods.

"I did, Margo, I did."

"Can we hear it?" she asks.

"Oh, you don't want to hear my attempt. Yours are so much better."

"We do!" says Margo.

"Read it," says Flo. "Please."

"OK," he says. "If you insist." He smiles as he says it and waves his hand in the air and grabs his blue book like he's quite excited to share.

"I've done one like Raj. It's by my cat."

I have a chair that is mine.
Well, it's not mine
But I use it a lot and the bigs say that's fine.
There are two bigs.
One is big.
The other is bigger.
They call me James Bond. I don't know why.
I own four things.
Two bowls, a rug and a straw mouse
That was wrapped under this big shiny tree thing
And the bigs made a fuss and attached it to string.
I chased it.

They gave me tuna.

So I chased it again.

They gave me more tuna.

So I chased it again.

And they ignored me.

I have my own door. I push it with my head.

The bigs put the door in for me.

They shouted a lot that day because it
was hard to cut the hole.

They shouted a lot the second day
because of Scarred Tom.

Scarred Tom lives two doors down.

His scars are battle scars.

His bigs go away a lot.

He steals and wanders around.

He has very sharp claws.

And jaws.

He came through the door.

The smaller big screamed.

Overreaction I'd say.

The bigger big laughed but tried to chase Tom out.

Except you don't really chase Scarred Tom.

He decides if he leaves.

But the broom made him decide to go.

The bigs went out.

They came back with a new door
and a bloomin' fancy collar
That I wear
So only I can open the door.
'Like James Bond's bow tie' the bigs said.
So I brought them a gift
A vole.
Lucky them.
Dead fresh.

Mr Froggatt closes his book.

"That was great," says India, clapping as if it's the best thing she's ever heard.

"Just a small ditty," says Mr Froggatt.

"I thought it had to rhyme," says Jack.

"Poems have no rules," says Mr Froggatt. "They just have to say what you want to say."

"Did James Bond eat the vole?" asks Jack.

"Not really…" says Mr Froggatt. "There's a funny story in that one, Jack."

"Tell us," says Flo.

"You know what?" says Mr Froggatt. "I'll do it as another poem. Is that OK?"

Flo nods and smiles and the bell rings. We pack up our things.

Philip pushes his chair back. It scrapes on the floor.

"It was about your cat really," says Philip. "Not your house."

Mr Froggatt looks at him and smiles. "I suppose it was, Philip. But that's OK. Poems can take you any which way."

Philip shrugs.

"I had five books back," says Mr Froggatt. "That's really pleasing. Have a go again tonight, you lot. Your books are here, with a new poem to write. If anyone else would like to try a new poem, just let me know! We'll share again next Friday."

The corridor outside fills with noise.

The vet's appointment is at four. My stomach churns. I'm shuffling out of my chair.

"Everyone has a letter too," says Mr Froggatt. "Take one from the pile. It's about the high-school welcome evening."

We tuck our chairs in. My laces catch under the chair leg. I'm hot and my tummy is tight now.

"James." I turn to look at Mr Froggatt. He's handing me my blue book. "I liked it." I take the book. "Everything all right?" he says.

I nod and follow Tomaz out of the classroom.

No, everything is not all right.

Nothing is all right.

"Will you share yours next time?" says Tomaz but I can't talk.

I just shrug and say, "Maybe. I've got to go."

I grab my bag from my peg and run out of school. Mum is there, with Digger. He sees me and wags his tail and his body curves in joy.

I nestle into him.

"You OK?" says Mum.

"Yep," I say.

"We'll go straight there. Do your laces."

I bend down and shove them inside my shoes.

We walk round the corner and Mum gets out her keys and opens the car boot. Digger jumps in and I attach his lead to the silver hook.

"He thinks he's off to the forest," I say.

"Perhaps we could take him after," says Mum. "Let him roll in that muddy water he loves."

I climb in. We are quiet. Digger rests his head on the back of the seat. There is a lot of traffic.

"We can't be late," I say.

"We won't be," says Mum.

"The petrol light is on," I say. "Why didn't you fill up?"

"We have enough," says Mum.

"We should have told Dad," I say.

"We will," says Mum. "But not yet. It's probably nothing."

The vet's is busy. Mum knows the lady behind the counter. They went to school together. Her name is Jacinda. It's written on a big badge pinned to her top.

"Take a seat," says Jacinda. "It won't be long."

There are two other dogs, a bird in a cage and a cat, crouched low in its carry pen. The owner of the cat is on her phone, laughing. I can't even smile right now.

We sit on the plastic chairs and wait. There are posters about lungworm and fleas and ways to protect pets in the hot weather.

I nudge Mum. "Digger has all the stuff for those things, doesn't he?"

"Yes," says Mum. "Of course." But she looks at the posters and I can tell she's thinking about it.

Another cat comes in. They are told to go in the 'cats' corner'. There are raised levels for the baskets and a sign that says, 'Cats like to be up high, off the floor'. I feel a bit worried about the cat in the carry pen. I want to tell the owner to get off the phone and put her cat up high.

The nurse comes out. "Buster, please," she says.

It's the tiny dog with the diamond collar. The owner lifts him up and tucks him under her arm.

Mum nudges me. "Remember when we could carry

Digger like that?"

I smile and say, "In the red jumper."

And Mum smiles and sniffs quite hard and looks out of the window as if the memory of the red jumper is just a little too much.

Digger lies down to wait, his legs stretched out.

"He's lovely," says the man with the bird.

And then a different nurse comes out and asks for the bird. It's called Chirpy.

"Hardly original," says Mum, when they've gone. "Cute though." She picks up a leaflet about puppy training. I feel a bit sick, sitting here waiting. The room is very quiet now. The lady on the phone taps away, still smiling. I look at the clock. They are running late.

Buster comes back out. He's walking now, his tiny paws slipping on the tiled floor.

"Jacinda will give you the tablets," says the nurse. "Just two a day and come back if you're at all worried."

I clench my fist tight and hope so hard that Digger will just need two tablets a day.

The nurse looks down at her notes. "Digger next, please," she says, and we stand up and Digger jumps to his feet and pulls towards Buster, sniffing the tiny dog's behind.

We follow the nurse into the vet's office.

"Hi," says the vet. "I'm Charlie." He leans straight down

to Digger. "Hello, gorgeous! Aren't you just lovely?" He glances at his computer. "OK, Digger, let's see how you're doing. Front right leg, yes?"

Charlie feels the lump, feels the leg, feels Digger all over. Takes his temperature. Looks in his mouth, asks about his general health. Mum and Charlie talk about parking problems and how good it is that the vet's practice is next to the butcher's shop. They even laugh about sausage rolls for lunch. I want to scream at them to just focus on Digger. And then Charlie stops and rests back on the counter.

"I'm not sure what it is," he says.

All that and he's not sure. Maybe if they talked less about sausage rolls, he might have more of an idea.

"We need to remove it and then, once the lump is out, we can have it tested and see what we're dealing with."

Digger sits back and pants. I move close to him and rub his paw in the way he likes.

"Could it be an infection or a fatty lump?" asks Mum. She really does believe every word Dave says.

"Possibly," says Charlie. He strokes Digger. "He's young and strong. That's all in his favour."

He turns to the computer, entering the details, planning times and appointments, talking with Mum about when to bring Digger in.

"Will he be OK?" I say. "He has to be OK. Is it cancer?"

Mum blinks hard. "James," she says. "Let's not go there."

"Could it be?" I say to Charlie.

He kneels down next to me and Digger. "I really don't know right now, James. We will do everything we can to help him though, OK? He is in the best hands." He stands up again and goes back to the screen. "Monday at nine, then?" he says to Mum.

"Why Monday?" I say. "That's almost three days. Why can't we do it right now? Or tomorrow."

"James," says Mum, resting her hand on my shoulder. She looks at Charlie. "Monday is the soonest, yes?"

Charlie nods. "The absolute soonest. We don't do these procedures on the weekend and he needs to come in with an empty tummy. Try not to worry, guys. Let's just see what Monday brings."

We leave the room and go to the desk. Digger takes a big drink from the water bowl and then lies down. He's so good. He doesn't deserve any of this.

"Shall we pay today or Monday?" asks Mum.

"Monday," says Jacinda. She is tapping away on the computer. "Can I just check the address is Bounty Road?"

"No," Mum says. "That's my ex's address."

"Maybe we just have that for the insurance."

"I have no idea why," says Mum. "We've never used that address. Everything should come to me."

Jacinda twists her necklace. "Let me check again."

"Dad and I brought him that time in half-term when he had the tick," I say.

Jacinda taps away again. "Maybe that's it," she says. "We can sort it all out on Monday. You can use the insurance for this as it will definitely be over the excess."

Mum nods and signs some paperwork.

"Just doesn't make sense," she mutters. Her lips are pulled into an angry line and her eyes are going, squeezing tight. She's about to cry.

Jacinda's seen it too. She comes round to our side of the desk and holds her arm. "Don't worry, Jackie," she says. "Digger is in the best hands."

I don't want to hear that again. I want to hear that everything is OK.

"I know," says Mum, with a sharp sniff. "Thanks."

I want to say, *It's not Digger. It's my dad. My dad left my mum for Kathy. Nothing has been right since then. And now she thinks Dad is trying to take Digger.* But instead I say, "What's insurance?"

Jacinda turns to me and strokes Digger. "A very clever thing, James. You pay a little into an account each month and then if something expensive has to be done, or an animal needs treatment, then the insurance pays for it. You just pay a small amount towards the cost, called the excess."

She pats Digger on his side.

"What's the excess?" asks Mum.

Jacinda goes back behind the desk and looks at her screen. "You'll need to double check with your insurer but it's normally something like this. It's not too bad," she says and she shows Mum the numbers she has in front of her.

Mum winces a bit.

"Lucky it's just that," she says.

"Right," says Jacinda, leaning over the desk to look at Digger. "We will see you on Monday, gorgeous hound!"

"Yes, thanks," says Mum and she rustles for her keys and pulls Digger's lead to get him up.

"But I'll be in school," I say. "I want to be with him."

"You can't, love, sorry," says Mum. "I know it's hard but you can pick him up with me, OK? I think Dave's free on Monday morning. He can come with me."

"Dave isn't his owner," I say. "We need to tell Dad."

We move towards the door.

"We will. Soon. Come on."

We get to the car. Digger jumps straight in.

"Shall we take him to the forest," I ask, "to roll in the mud?"

"I think he's tired," says Mum. "And it's raining." She turns on the windscreen wipers to try and make the specks of drizzle look like rain. She doesn't want to go any more.

I look out of the window on the way home and watch the town flash by. Mum turns the music on. She takes in a deep breath, like she does when Gena comes round and they sit together and do the cross-legged breathing thing.

I think of Digger as a puppy, wrapped in Mum's red jumper. He chewed it in the end, took it in the garden and rolled around, gnashing it until the red threads scattered across the lawn. We kept finding them for ages, those red threads. And then I remember the blue book and Mr Froggatt saying how much he liked my poem. I reach down into my school bag and pull it out.

I like my house.
There is a fruit tree in the garden
With stones in the winter
And fruit in the summer
And branches that fork and grow
And leaves that flutter, high and low.

Mr Froggatt has written a few comments.

I'd like to meet Digger. Does he bark?

I unzip the top pocket of my bag and find a pencil and reply.

Only in the dark

Can you sit on any branches or do they break?

I used to. Now they're too thin. Or maybe I'm too big and heavy.

Mr Froggatt has set a new poem.

INSECTS
I don't like insects
Do you?
I was bitten by a spider once
Spiders should live in the zoo.

Mum's phone rings. She glances quickly to see who it is. "Shall I answer it?" I say.

"NO," says Mum.

"Who is it?"

"Your father."

"Will you tell him about Digger?"

She doesn't answer. We stop at the traffic lights. She yanks on the handbrake, hard.

"He doesn't need to know. Digger will be fine," says Mum.

The rain is falling a little harder now. It's loud on the windows. Digger sits up and puts his head on the back seat.

"He should know," I say quietly.

"I'm just so mad he changed Digger's contact details. I wondered why I hadn't had any reminders for his worming tablets. They always text when he's due to take them. I need to check on that tomorrow."

I rub my window, tracing a pattern in the mist.

"Dad misses Digger," I say. "Maybe he wants to take care of him too."

The traffic lights change.

"Maybe," says Mum. The 'maybe' is harsh and bitter. She revs the car to set off. "And maybe I'm Cinderella."

Saturday 9th June

The pet-shop trip is Dave's idea.

"Let's cheer Digger up," he says, as if he knows what makes Digger happy. I don't think he's bothered about Digger. He's trying to make up with Mum. She's cross with him because of the new TV box he bought.

"Always said I'd never have this," she had muttered, staring at the hundreds of new channels on the screen as Dave set it up. "All this rubbishy stuff."

Well, Mum, you shouldn't have let Dave move in. Then none of this rubbishy stuff would be here.

"Digger would like the forest more," I say. "He loves playing in the mud."

But Dave wants to go to the pet shop and then get a burger. I think he just wants the burger.

We get in Mum's car. Digger's excited. He loves going in the car. But when Dave starts the engine, the petrol-warning light flashes at double speed.

"Not again," says Dave.

"We'll have to go in the van," says Mum.

"It's full of Mrs Dawson's old bathroom," says Dave. "We can't take Digger in the back."

"Well," says Mum. "Digger will have to stay at home then." She gets out and slams the door.

"But this trip is about Digger," calls Dave. He rubs his head as if he's not sure what to do. And it's odd because at that moment I feel a bit bad for Dave. It would all be fine if Mum had just put petrol in the car. I open the door and get out.

Mum is opening the boot. "Put Digger back inside please, James," she says and she turns and walks up the path and starts pulling dead heads off the lavender.

Digger doesn't want to get out. He just sits there, rock solid. I pull and pull on his lead but he won't budge. Dave goes back in the house to get his keys for the van. I call his name. Which is really odd because I never use Dave's name. He spins back round.

"Can you bring a bit of ham, to tempt Digger out?" I ask.

Mum throws the dead flower heads behind the pot and then snaps off more. I wrap my arms around Digger's neck and bury my head in his ears.

Dave comes back out with a large piece of ham. He passes it to me and Digger jumps straight out, gobbles it down, licks his chops.

"Take him in, James," says Dave. "Let's go and get him a treat and then we'll take him to the forest later."

I stop for a second. I don't like Dave telling me what to do but I have nothing to say so I take Digger indoors. When I come back out, Mum and Dave are in the van, both facing forwards, not talking. I open the side door and climb in. The seats are black and hot and squidgy.

Dave starts the van. The radio blasts on so he turns it down.

"You should put petrol in when it's half full," says Dave, "rather than risking it."

"Will you just leave it?" says Mum.

I don't think I've ever seen Dave and Mum cross with each other before. And it's odd. Because I don't like it.

Dave puts his seat belt on and we do the same. It's hard to find the seat belts in the van. They get stuck in the seats. You have to twist round and yank them out. But I think we're all happy to have something to do.

We drive in silence for a while and then Dave puts on the radio and reaches for Mum's hand. They sit like that all along the main road until Dave has to turn right and lets go of her hand. But then Mum rests it on his knee instead.

"Thanks for letting me get the TV package," he says. I wonder if mentioning that will make her more cross.

But Mum squeezes his leg.

"It's your home too," she says. "I know the football is important to you. And I'm sure James and I will find something good to watch."

A stupid love song comes on. Dave pretends to sing it to Mum. She rests her head on his shoulder.

"I'll never get used to that remote control though," says Mum.

"Yeah, you will," says Dave. He wraps his hand in hers. "Just like you got used to me."

There's something sticky under my leg. I reach under and pull out a Cornish pasty wrapper. It has bits of gravy stuck on the rim.

"Yuck," says Mum.

"Oh, that's Jim's," says Dave. "Sorry, mate. Jim always has his Friday pasty." He takes the wrapper from me and throws it in the back. "And his Monday pasty. And Wednesdays too." I turn my head sharp, so Dave can't see my mouth twitch. "Not Thursday though. That's giant sausage-roll day." I bend right down and bite my smile away. "Eat one in the shop and the second comes free. And Jim, always, without fail, gets the second one."

Mum's giggling as if Dave has just won comedian of the year.

We trundle along, the tools rattling and shaking. There is

a coil of white plastic by my feet. I look in the back of the van. Dave's right. There isn't any space for Digger. Unless he sat in the bath and we tied his lead to the taps.

There is an old toilet right behind me and it smells.

We go over speed bumps and the whole van shakes and the bath bumps up and down. And just at that moment I think about something that I don't like. Uncle Bobby would have liked Dave. They both love football. They would have found the same things funny. Mum laughs with Dave like she used to laugh with Uncle Bobby.

We turn into the big shopping centre car park, past the bowling alley and the cinema. There is a giant advert for a new spy thriller.

"Great, that film is out," says Dave. "I'd love to go." He glances sideways, trying to catch my eye. "The new TV package has lots of good movie channels too."

"Yes, that's a bonus, love, isn't it?" says Mum.

"This toilet smells," I say. But not very loud and they don't hear.

Mum and Dave walk up and down the aisles holding hands, putting chews and toys into a basket. I wander off, past the rabbits and hamsters and fish. On one shelf, there is a glass tank and a sign saying 'Indian/Common stick insect'. I look hard. And then I spot them, hanging upside down, like twigs. How cool to have the ultimate camouflage, to look just like the thing you live on.

If I could look like the thing I live on, I would be my bed. I love my bed. With Digger right there. Mum would be a bush in the garden. She always says that's her happy place, out in the garden, weeding and pruning and trying to beat the slugs. And Dave, well, Dave would be a football, an old squidgy one with no air and two furry eyebrows sticking out of the top.

Mum comes over.

"You think he'll like this?" She's holding a plastic duck. It squeaks.

I shake my head and grab a rubber bone from a stand and plonk it in her basket.

"Great choice, love," she says.

It is sometimes very easy to make Mum happy.

Dinner tonight is a 'movie dinner'. Apparently it's the new Saturday night thing. Dave is scrolling through the choices and keeps turning to me, looking hopeful. I shake my head, over and over. I've seen all his suggestions. With Dad.

Mum's right. This thing is a waste of time.

"Let's try this trailer," Dave says. "*The Diplodocus Returns*. What's not to like?"

Digger is by my feet, lying very still. I stroke his head. It seems Digger is allowed to stay for 'movie dinners'. No banishment to the utility room tonight.

"*The Diplodocus ... extinct ... forever. Not one left on the island. Until now ... until today ... until the discovery of one remaining egg ... still warm.*"

I yawn.

Dave fumbles with the control. "Maybe not," he says. "What about this one?"

The trailer starts with a huge ball of fire. And then the sound of gun shots.

That's more like it, Dave.

"*Darkness. Fear. Fire. Just one woman able to save the world.*" I love the voiceover guy. "*If she can stay alive...*"

Blood splatters across the screen. This looks good.

But then Mum bustles in with peanuts. "No way," she says. "Far too violent."

Dave sighs and returns to the movie list, flicking through the titles. "Here we go," he says, picking a new one. "Perfect. Jacks, watch the trailer. Think you'll like it." He often calls her Jacks. No one else has ever called Mum Jacks. She is Jackie.

"*Two worlds at war. Two robots programmed to kill. Two humans with a crime to avenge…*"

"Horrid," says Mum.

Have to give it to Dave, this one looks OK.

"Oh, I forgot my wine," says Mum and she leaves the room.

"Just wait," says Dave, hitting pause and turning to talk to me as if we are in this together. "It's got her favourite actor! She told me –" he scoops up a fistful of peanuts and tips them into his mouth – "that she's seen every movie this guy's been in."

I didn't know Mum had a favourite actor. I look at Dave, picking the peanuts that missed his mouth off his jumper, and I feel kind of glad he knows that about Mum.

Mum comes back in, glass in hand. "Let's see then." She sits down next to me and slides her foot under Digger's tummy.

Dave presses play. The music booms and the actor takes off his leather jacket and strides around the laboratory, testing out gadgets.

Mum leans forwards and takes some peanuts from the bowl and says, "OK, but only if it's a twelve rating."

Dave turns and winks at me and I smile and make a yes fist and then Dave turns away to press the play button and I feel a bit strange about giving him the yes fist and the smile.

It's only a stupid movie.

Sunday 10th June

<u>INSECTS</u>

There's a flea
In my tea
And another on my knee.
There's a spider
Inside 'er
Like a racing driver.
Scorpions bite
At night.
I wouldn't fight.
My house has ants
But not in my pants.
Stick insects are pets
Do they go to the vet's?
How would a vet find a stick insect's heart?
It must be hard to take a stick insect apart.

Monday 11th June

Mum is standing at the normal place by the school gate. The sun is shining, bouncing off everything.

"Did they call?" I ask.

"Yes, we can get him now."

"What is it?"

"We won't know yet," says Mum.

I stop and throw my bag down.

"What do you mean? I thought we would find out today!"

"Pick up your bag, James. We need to go."

I grab the bag and follow her to the car.

"It will take a few days for the results to come through. Stop thinking the worst."

"Don't say that to me. Not after Uncle Bobby. At that enquiry thing with the doctors, Dad said they should have tested sooner and they sort of agreed."

Mum stops walking and pulls me gently into the end of a driveway, out of the stream of kids. She lays her hand on my cheek.

"This is completely different, James. I don't want you being scared like that. Uncle Bobby had a cancer that came on very fast. You know that. You can't compare. OK?" She pulls me in to her. My cheek rubs her T-shirt and I can smell her perfume. I want to be hugged but I can hear the other kids close by. I want to cry but I can't. "Now," says Mum, "let's go and get Digger and spoil him rotten." I take a deep breath and nod.

We join the parade of kids again and reach the car. It's hot. I get in and when Mum starts the engine, we put the windows down.

Tomaz walks past and leans in. "Is Digger OK?"

"Just going to get him now," I say and I put my belt on.

Tomaz waves and runs off.

"Did you tell Dad?" I ask as Mum joins the line of traffic.

"Not yet," says Mum. "No need right now."

"Digger is Dad's dog too."

Mum sighs and speaks very slowly, as if I'm learning English. "Digger lives with us and is our dog. Your dad does not live with us. We will take care of Digger."

I know when to be quiet. Now is not the time to argue.

We go to the butcher's first, which seems a bit odd. Mum wants to get sausages for tea. She says I can choose something. But I don't want anything. We have to wait ages to pay. I pull Mum's wrist to look at her watch.

"We've got loads of time," says Mum.

She puts the sausages in her bag and we leave. She stops outside the vet's door.

"Digger will have a big cone on – to stop him chewing the wound."

"I know that," I say. But I didn't and the thought of Digger wearing a cone makes my breath go into little, sharp puffs.

We go inside and walk straight up to the front desk. Jacinda is there.

"Hey, guys," she says, smiling. "Good to see you."

Mum says hi and then she turns to me. "You sit down there. Have a chat to that sweet little dog." There is the ugliest mutt sitting on an old man's lap. It is growling, a low, faint growl.

"I'm all right," I say.

"I just want to sort the paperwork," says Mum.

"You mean you want to check Dad's address isn't on the stuff any more."

She sighs. "Sort of."

The door flies open and the largest, fluffiest dog I've ever seen comes in. Drops of drool hang from its mouth.

"Now, *that's* a dog," says Mum. "What breed?"

"This is Alaska," says the owner. "She's a Newfoundland."

Alaska almost reaches my shoulder. She turns to me and pushes my side.

"She likes you," says the owner.

I pat her head.

Mum has moved to the end of the counter. She is talking to Jacinda, flicking through pieces of paper.

"Is Alaska sick?" I ask.

"No, but she has been," says the lady. "She's all better now. We're just here for a check-up."

"Oh," I say.

"Are you here with a pet?" she asks.

"My dog," I say. "Digger. He has a lump. Well, he doesn't have it any more."

"That's good," she says, and I nod, but I don't know if anything is good right now.

"Say hi to Digger from us," says the lady and she pulls Alaska away and I stroke her black fur as she leaves my side.

I look over at Mum. She is shaking her head, running her hand through her hair. I go to her.

"What's wrong?" I say.

"Nothing, nothing at all," says Mum. She turns to Jacinda. "We'll sort it. Thank you." Her lips are a thin line.

"Is it Digger? What's wrong?" I say again.

"Digger's great. Charlie is bringing him out soon."

She turns back to the desk. "The address is sorted now though, yes?"

"All sorted," says Jacinda.

A door opens at the back and Charlie comes out. He has Digger on the lead. Digger sees us and pulls madly, his claws scraping on the tiles, the cone bashing against the wall to his side. I kneel next to him and wrap myself around him, my face scraping the white plastic. He smells different, of cleaning things and medicine but I lean inside the cone and he licks my face and life feels OK again.

"How many days for the results?" says Mum.

"About a week," says Charlie. "I've sent the samples off to the lab already. You can pay a bit extra and get the results quicker if you want. We'll have answers soon. I got good clearance."

"What's clearance?" I ask.

"I managed to get all of the lump," says Charlie. "Try not to worry. I'll call you when I hear from the lab."

"We need to know as soon as possible," I say. I tug on Mum's sleeve. "I'll pay. My money box is full and I have that savings thing Gran pays my pocket money in to."

"A week will be fine," says Mum. She squeezes my hand.

Digger lifts a paw on to Mum's leg. But it's the poorly leg and he puts it straight down again. And then he tries to nestle into her but he can't because of the big plastic cone round his neck. He makes a little sound. Mum bends low and tickles Digger's nose. He likes that. And then she stands up and looks at me and then Charlie.

"We'll pay the extra," says Mum.

Charlie smiles and nods.

"Thought you might," he says and he asks Jacinda to sort it.

I like Charlie. Maybe Charlie could date Mum. A vet would be really useful to have around. Much more useful than Dave. All Dave's done is fix the leaking toilet.

"Are you parked outside?" says Charlie. He comes with us to the car. "Let's just support him as he jumps in," he says. "But don't worry about the wound. It's stitched up tight."

Mum opens the boot. Charlie supports Digger's tummy to give him a boost and Digger jumps in. "See you soon, Digger!" he says as he gives him a final pat and then goes back inside the vet's. Mum watches him go.

"He's great, isn't he?" I say.

"Wonderful," says Mum, clipping Digger in. "Let's go." She heads round to her door.

I stroke Digger and pull his blanket straight. I take a peep at his leg. There is a white dressing. They have shaved a patch of fur. I didn't know they would shave his fur.

"Come on," says Mum as she starts the engine. "We can

cook those sausages. I bought extra for Digger."

I put the boot down. I can just reach it now, if I stand on tiptoe.

Digger looks at me through the glass, his golden face in a circle of white plastic, his brown eyes staring at mine.

Tuesday 12th June

Mr Froggatt is taking the afternoon assembly. He is standing at the front of the hall with a big black bag, tapping his feet.

"He looks a bit hot," says Tomaz, nudging me.

I think Mr Froggatt is nervous. I don't want him to feel nervous. He claps his hands and waits for us all to quieten down.

We are sitting on the chairs at the back. It's a Year 6 privilege. Philip is stretched out, his legs crossed in front of him.

Mr Edwards taps him on the shoulder. "Sit up," he whispers.

But Philip ignores him. He always ignores Mr Edwards. I think Mr Froggatt has seen. He stares at Philip and then he asks for helpers. The Year 3 children all raise their hands. He picks one person from each year and from Year 6 he picks Philip. Philip didn't ask to be picked. He doesn't look happy.

Mr Froggatt talks about friendship. He asks the four helpers to join him and choose one shoe from the bag and then put it on the table. The Year 3 girl takes out a smart black polished shoe. The Year 4 boy takes out a slipper. The Year 5 girl takes out a trainer and then Philip pulls out a muddy football boot. He holds it with a thumb and one finger.

"Yeah, I wouldn't go too close," says Mr Froggatt.

Philip pretends it smells really bad and everyone laughs.

"Thank you, Philip," says Mr Froggatt in a very loud voice. "Maybe you'd like to go back to Year Six now."

Philip puts the boot down quickly and it falls off the table and the studs clatter on the floor. Everyone laughs again and then Philip comes back to the chairs and sits down. Mr Froggatt tells the other children to go back to their places. He waits to check Philip is sitting properly and then he carries on.

He picks up the trainer. "This is Martin." We laugh. "Well, it's not Martin. But it's just like my friend Martin. I'm completely comfortable with Martin. He's my best friend. I can be with him all the time. We can go anywhere together and it works. Having Martin in my life is a wonderful thing."

Then Mr Froggatt holds up the smart black shoe. "This," he says, "is Kevin." We all laugh again. "Kevin and I see each other every few months. We are often at parties together. Kevin is very, very funny. He is loud and I like him. But there is no way I could be with him all the time. Just like I couldn't wear this shoe all the time. It rubs a bit on the heel."

I think my black shoe is Jack.

Mr Froggatt's slipper is the friend he turns to when he needs comfort. Her name is Helen and he has known her all his life. She's a very good listener and he feels totally at ease with her. I think of Mum's friend Gena. Maybe she's a slipper.

The football boot is Mr Froggatt's tennis partner, Benedict. He is very bossy and brags a lot and if Mr Froggatt misses an easy shot, he tuts. Very loudly. But they play well together and often win difficult matches.

"Think about all your friends," says Mr Froggatt. "Value each friend in their own special way. If you have a trainer like Martin in your life, then you are very lucky indeed. But you also need slippers and football boots and party shoes."

Tomaz and I stare straight ahead. Neither of us moves or says anything. But I think we both know we are each other's trainer.

Mr Froggatt looks very happy when the assembly is over. We are the last class to leave the hall.

"That got me thinking," says Freya as we walk back to class.

"That's the aim!" says Mr Froggatt.

We all find our desks.

"Just five minutes until the bell," says Mr Froggatt. "Anyone have any news to share?"

"Is it ready?" asks India. "The poem. You did promise, Mr Froggatt. We want to find out about the vole."

Mr Froggatt looks around for his blue book. "It is, India," he says, holding it up. "Shall I read it now?" We all say yes. He leans on his desk, like he always does. "Anyone who isn't into voles, please feel free to read your own book."

But we listen.

Every one of us.

I gave them a gift, a beautiful vole
Fresh and furry, just yanked from its hole.
I carried it carefully and hopped through my flap
And thought I'd be greeted with cheers and a clap,
Thought they'd be thrilled at such a day's work
But the two great big scaredys went truly berserk.
A screech from big one, from big two a great roar
As he grabbed for the broom and bashed at the floor.
That's what I got for my hard-fought prize,
Screaming and yelling and frightened wide eyes.
So I dropped it right there, on the kitchen floor,
Big one grabbed me and shoved me out through my door.

93

The flap flapped madly, I turned to just see
My prize, my vole, scuttle off free.
Big one and big two yelled in despair,
"Shut the door, seal that off, it's under the chair!"
I sat by the window, with the best seat in town
As the two great buffoons tried to hunt the vole down.
There were towels under doorways and boxes galore,
A line of Tupperware lined up near each door.
"I've got it! I've trapped it!" shouted big one,
Lifted the box and the vole was gone.
"It's there, right there!" screeched big two with a spade
Held aloft on the hilarious trap they had made.
Down came the tool, cracked the floor with its weight
And out popped the vole not a moment too late.
It scuttled away, healthy and plump
And the two bigs collapsed in chairs in a slump.
"We're done, we've failed, we gave it our best
but we can't sleep in a house with a rodent pest.
There's only one thing for it, I know what we need,
The best special agent to take on the deed."
They were quiet for a moment, then a flood of light
As the door opened wide and they stared out at the night.
A saucer of tuna, the treat box to rattle
and off they started with their stupid prattle,
"James Bond, James Bond, we love you, look here

Your favourite treats, an endless supply, sweet dear.
Come in, we're sorry, we need your great skill,
Please chase down that vole and complete the kill."
Hmmm, I considered, part of me ready to jump
At the thought of that prey, so juicy and plump,
But I didn't quite like being shoved back outside
While my vole sat and watched my disappearing backside.
If the other cats knew, I'd be laughed out of my patch,
Hardly the scariest, most vicious catch.
But behind me, in the bushes, I can hear old Scarred Tom,
He's on the lookout for trouble and I'm the chosen one.
It was Daisy last night, Tom had sharpened his claws,
And now she's limping slowly on only three paws.
And Boot's bushy tail, like a fox before he caught her,
Is now wrapped in bandages and six inches shorter.
Scarred Tom is whining, he's up on the fence,
My tail flicks high and my claws grow tense.
Mustn't show the bigs that I'm scared to the core,
So I stretch just a little and amble up to the door.
Have a nibble of tuna and accept the gentle lift,
I'm back through my door, I've escaped Tom's night shift.
It doesn't look like home, it's a disaster scene,
They'll be up all night getting this place clean.
And then I hear it, a scuttle and a frantic scratch,
Let the chaos ensue, vole! You've now met your match.

Mr Froggatt closes his book.

"Wow!" says India.

"It rhymed," says Jack.

"Yes, that one did," says Mr Froggatt.

The bell rings.

"Did he eat it?" asks Eva.

"I've really no idea," says Mr Froggatt. "But we never saw it again! Have a lovely afternoon, all."

Everyone stands to go. Mr Froggatt passes me my blue book.

"I loved it, James," he says. He says it very quietly and without anyone noticing. "Try the next one."

I wander out to the corridor and open the book.

How would a vet find a stick insect's heart?
It must be hard to take a stick insect apart.

Good question! I looked it up – their organs float in their blood – yuck!

CLOTHING
What's your favourite thing to wear?
Jumper, coat, pyjamas?
I like best my grandpa hat
It drives my wife bananas.

Swimming is cancelled. The pool is closed.

"They send a message. They said they clean it," says Tomaz's mum. She is dropping me straight home. I still get the good food though. "I don't know why they do that now," she says.

"I think I know," I say. I bite into the huge pastry with cream on top.

"Why?" says Tomaz.

I lean over to him and whisper, "I bet a little kid has done a number two."

He spits out his pastry, all over the seat in front.

"What's this two thing?" asks Tomaz's mum.

Tomaz says something in Polish. His mum nods as if his answer makes perfect sense.

"What did you say?"

He lowers his voice, "That they do it two times a year, to really keep the pool clean. She'd never let me swim again if she knew!"

"Good idea," says Tomaz's mum. "I saw plaster go by last time."

Tomaz and I have to bend over to stop laughing so hard.

MY FAVOURITE THING TO WEAR

Red football jumper
Liverpool FC
My Uncle Bobby gave it to me
On my ninth birthday
Left it once in a café
Dad and I had to drive all the way back to get it
Mum was really cross because we were late back
and it was her turn to have me.
Like I'm a chess piece.

Wednesday 13th June

Digger has cancer.

The lump wasn't an infection or a fatty thing. The lump is nasty and Digger has cancer.

Dave was wrong.

Dave is always wrong.

He is wrong, wrong, wrong.

"They're pretty sure it can be treated, James," says Mum. "Are you listening?" She strokes my hair. It's the only bit of me she can reach. I'm curled up in a ball on the sofa with all the cushions piled around me. I want all this to go away. I want to ask so many things but no words will come. "Charlie is going to talk to a clever cancer vet who will advise us on the right treatment. Digger has to have a few more tests done on Friday. It's what they call a malignant tumour but they are confident it can be treated."

She peels a few cushions away.

I find a mumbly, spitty, all-words-the-same-way kind

of voice. "Charlie said he got it all. He said he had that clearing thing." I push myself deeper into the cushions.

I can hear the cars outside, the clock ticking.

"He did," says Mum. "But we need to make sure that if anything broke away, or he missed a tiny bit, that we catch everything. Give Digger the best bet for a full recovery. His chances are good. He'll have as much treatment as he needs."

His chances are good.

It makes Digger sound like a weather report.

I wonder if Uncle Bobby ever had a good chance.

"Charlie said you did really well finding the lump, under all that bloomin' fur."

I still can't make the words.

"This is nothing like Uncle Bobby's cancer," says Mum. "Nothing at all." It's like Mum knows what I want to ask. She stays next to me. Very close. She takes another cushion away. "And Digger knows nothing about this. He feels exactly the same. He needs you to love him just the same."

"More," I mutter.

"Pardon, love?" she says.

I yell it this time. "More. I'll love him more!"

"OK," she says. "Well, that will be the best way."

I hear the front door bang shut. And then I hear Dave, calling out Mum's name like he owns the house. His keys land in the bowl and then I hear Digger rustle through, his cone scraping the wall, greeting Dave.

"Hey," says Dave. "How's my favourite dog?"

I want to rip the cushions apart. I bet he's kneeling down, stroking him, running his hand down the side of the cone to tickle him under the chin. Like he cares. As if. As if he cares.

"Does Dave know?" I flip a cushion over and stare at Mum. "Did he know before me?"

"Yes," she says, softly but firmly. "He was here when Charlie rang. And I was upset and a bit tearful so Dave had to talk to him." I glare at her and pull the cushion back over my face.

"In here, Dave," says Mum quietly, as if to make sure I know that being with me is more important than seeing Dave. Which I don't believe.

"Hey," says Dave. "How we all doing?" I can smell his overalls. He sits on the sofa. I want to kick him. I want to stick my leg out from behind the cushions and kick him. Digger is with him. He nuzzles under the cushions. The big plastic cone moves them like a snowplough. And then he is with me, climbing on me, licking my chin, my face rubbing on the cone. We are in our own little tunnel of plastic.

"I'll have a shower," says Dave. "And then how about fish and chips?"

"Brilliant idea," says Mum. "Fancy that, James?"

I shrug. I don't care. I don't want to eat.

"I need to phone Dad," I say. "Does he know?"

Mum fiddles with Digger's cone, checks the fastenings and makes sure it's not too tight.

"Yes, yes, he does," she says.

She glances at Dave and he nods.

"Good stuff," says Dave and he stands up. "I'll have that shower." He leans down and kisses Mum. "Sean's not coming tonight. Thought it best."

"OK," says Mum.

"I want to talk to Dad," I say.

"That's fine," says Mum.

"Later," I say. I didn't think she'd want me to. I'm not actually in the mood. "I'll call him after tea."

Mum wraps herself around Digger and she is close to crying, I can tell. "You daft old mutt," she says and then she pulls herself up and leaves for the kitchen.

Dad calls me. We are finishing dinner when the landline rings. Mum answers it and then passes me the phone.

"It's your dad," she says.

Dave scoops out some ice cream from the tub and plonks it in his bowl.

I take the phone and go into the lounge.

"Hi," I say.

"Hey, James. How you doing?"

"Not great," I say.

"Really sorry, love, about Digger. Your mum told me."

"Will you come and see him?"

"I can't, James, you know that. I'm working away tonight. Like I told you. Or we'd be together. I'll see you and Digger in a few days' time though."

"I think he may need worming tablets."

"Um, OK. I can talk to your mum about that."

"We mustn't get things mixed up. You know, with the paperwork."

"No, I know," says Dad.

"Can you talk to—" and then I stop. I can hear Kathy calling his name, over and over as if she's not sure which room he's in. My breath catches. I feel sick. He's right there, at home.

"I thought you were away tonight," I say.

"I'm about to go, love. I'm just packing the car and then I'm off down to London."

I flop on to the sofa, the relief racing through me. Kathy calls again. It's a shriek this time. I want Dad to tell Kathy to go away.

I wait. I'm quiet.

"I better go," says Dad.

"OK," I say, and I hang up. And then I feel bad. We never end calls like that. I sit up and push the address button and scroll through to find his number. It's under Peter J. Like he's the builder or the guy who fixes the TV. It rings. Two or three rings and then he answers. I'm so relieved. He must have been waiting, wondering if he should call back. Feeling the same as me.

"I love you, Dad," I say.

"Oh, hi, James." It's Kathy. Kathy has answered Dad's phone. Dad moved on that fast. I don't like Kathy hearing me. I would never tell Dad I loved him in front of Kathy.

"I'll tell him," she says. "He's just putting his bag in the car."

I don't want to talk to her. I'm not sure what to say. I murmur a sort of OK noise.

"Is there anything else, James?" she says.

"No," I say. I have to force the word out.

"OK then, bye now," she says. She waits for a second but I don't reply and she hangs up.

Is there anything else?

Uh, yeah, he's my dad.

Who does she think she is? Miss Hoovering Queen. I wish she'd hoover herself up, and end up stuck in the big plastic drum. Come on, movie man. Do your best.

Kathy, a boring lady from a boring town ... until the demon hoover took over and she was the first to get sucked up the

104

tube... But how long could she survive in the plastic drum...

Mum calls me in for dessert. I put the phone back and sit down. Dave puts some ice cream in my bowl. I stir it round and round and round so it turns all whippy.

"We need to get Digger's worming tablets," I say.

"I know," says Mum. "I'm sorting it."

"Dad wants to see Digger."

Mum takes some strawberries from the bowl in the middle of the table and dishes them out.

"He will," she says. "On Friday."

"Are you going to your dad's on Friday?" says Dave.

"Yes," I say, jabbing a strawberry to bits. "Is that OK with you?"

"James," says Mum. "Don't talk to Dave like that."

"I forgot, mate," says Dave. "That's all."

Mum leans over to Dave and puts a hand on his arm.

"It's Peter's birthday," she says. "They're having a bit of a party."

"Are we not invited?" says Dave. He's smiling. "Maybe we'll turn up. I'll bring some of my mates, straight from the footie. I'll make sure Darren puts his teeth in."

Mum's giggling, her hand over her mouth. I'm trying *really* hard not to smile. I shove in some ice cream.

"And I won't let Jim have beans for his tea. You know how beans fill him with wind."

OK, so I have to smile. I have to. The ice cream sort of splutters a bit.

"Not sure Kathy would like Jim to fart near the cake."

"Do stop," says Mum, wiping her mouth.

Dave sits back, arms folded, smiling.

"Jim," says Dave, "has actually, in the past, farted out birthday candles."

I cough back my laughter, scraping the last of the ice cream from my bowl.

"I'm sure James will have fun," says Mum, shoving Dave gently to shut him up, but she's loving this. Dave making us both laugh. "He'll be with us the weekend after."

"No worries," says Dave. He starts to clear the table. "I'd booked to go bowling, mate, that's all. Thought it might cheer us all up. Another time, yeah?"

I shrug. I would definitely a thousand times rather go bowling than to the stupid party. But I'd never tell Dave that.

I go to my room with Digger and get out the blue book.

Mum was really cross because we were late back
and it was her turn to have me.
Like I'm a chess piece.

Great jumper! I support Man U though. Oh dear. Will you still talk to me?

That was kind of your Uncle Bobby. Does he buy you one every birthday?

I'm not sure what to put. I lift up my pencil and write:

I hate cancer.

There is a new poem on the next page.

FOOD
Baked beans, curry, spaggi bol with cheese
Burgers, French fries, carrots, mushy peas,
I love chocolate every day! Tell me what you love to eat
You never know, last day of term, it might be your favourite treat!

I'm not in the mood for poems tonight so I just snuggle down with Digger and watch YouTube. There's a guy on a tightrope, high over some mountains. The football twins are working their magic. There's a Minecraft forest with castles and lakes.

Digger twists round and tries to reach his leg. He wants to nuzzle the wound, pull at the stitches, but the cone is in his way. I take him downstairs and into the garden to play with the new bone. We have a game of tug. He shakes it in his mouth from side to side and it taps against the plastic. He wants more. It's good. He's forgotten about the stitches. I look around, through the patio doors to see if Mum can see. She is on the sofa with Dave, all cuddled up and talking.

I turn back to Digger. He is sniffing in the bushes. Then he lifts his leg and pees over Mum's plants and I have to smile because the force of the yellow stream actually tips the orange flower heads to one side, the pee flowing down the long green stems.

Thursday 14th June

FOOD

Bangers and mash, bangers and mash
If I had loads and loads of cash
That's what I'd buy
Bangers and mash.
With chocolate pud for pud
And if I really could
I'd have it every single day
If only I could find a way
I'd like to ditch the greens and fruit
Bangers and mash is the only loot.

Friday 15th June

"Let's see how many we have this week," says Mr Froggatt.

He pulls out nine poetry books.

India shares one about her favourite dress. It goes on and on and on. There's a whole page on how many colours it has. Flo has done one about her house.

"This is great," says Mr Froggatt. "And now Raj, a limerick on insects. Thanks for sharing."

There once was a scorpion called Bill
Who wanted to get more than his fill
So he stung his brothers,
chased away all the others
Until there was nothing left he could kill.

"Fab, Raj," says Mr Froggatt. "Well done, you!"

"Mum helped me," says Raj.

"Great. I like family efforts. The more ideas the better!"

I stare out of the window, listening, thinking of Digger, wanting it all to be OK. Wishing it all to be OK. He's there right now, with Charlie, having more tests.

"Last one to share today. Eva's. This'll make you chuckle."

My onesie, my onesie
Come to me, come to me
My onesie, my onesie
You're super ultra cosy
Like a teddy bear cuddle
Or wellies in a puddle
No elastic
No plastic
No zips
No clips
Onesie, oh, onesie
Come to me, come to me.

"I need to get one," says Mr Froggatt. "Sounds like the best thing to relax in after a long day with you lot."

"It really is," says Eva. "You can get grown-up ones."

"Maybe I'll make it the new teacher clothing," says Mr Froggatt. "Sure it will catch on. And uniform for you guys! It's the way ahead! What sort would you have?" We shout out our ideas. Tigers, flamingos, punk rockers.

"He's been really good," says Charlie. "We've tested his lymph nodes today and a few other areas. We'll send off the samples and have the results back next week. Then we can make a plan."

"Don't we need a plan now?" I ask. "We can't just keep testing him and not doing anything."

"The plan right now is to love him and spoil him," says Charlie. "Digger needs that." He looks at Mum. "I'll call when I know. Um ... we just need to talk about a few things at reception."

We go back to the front desk.

A little dog with pointy ears rushes over and the leads get tangled. Me and the dog's owner have to move away to twist the leads free. I look back at Mum. She is leaning over the counter, staring at the computer screen that Jacinda has tilted towards her. It's hard to hear what they're saying.

"... can't be the case... That's just impossible ... up to three hundred and fifty *already*..." She is rubbing her head and staring at the screen.

"Think about it over the weekend," says Jacinda. She has her head tipped in a funny way, as if she is trying to comfort Mum. "We can take it in stages."

Mum has gone a bit red. I think she might cry.

We leave the vet's and get into the car and drive home, the rain pouring down the windows.

"Is everything OK?" I ask. "What's three hundred and fifty? Is that to do with the cancer? What are we doing in stages? He has to have everything now."

"It's all fine. Digger will have whatever he needs to make him better."

At the sound of his name, Digger lifts up his head and rests it on the seat. He only has to wear the cone at night now.

"Did they find something bad with the node things?" I ask.

"No, James," says Mum, turning on the radio. "The results come next week. We just have to wait now. You know that. It's all fine."

I sit back and watch the wipers. It doesn't really feel fine.

"What time is Dad coming?" she asks.

I tip my head back and groan but only in my head, not so Mum can hear. I'm not in the mood for this party thing.

"Six, I think."

"Are you ready?"

"No."

"Do you have a present sorted?"

"Yep."

"Well done," says Mum.

"I'm hardly not going to give him a present, am I?"

She doesn't say anything.

"I could do with a bit of wrapping paper," I say.

"No problem," says Mum.

"Have you got him a card?" I ask. "Dad got one for you last birthday." It had gardening stuff on it. I helped him choose it. She had stared at it hard and passed it to Gena, who had tutted.

Dave had said, "That's nice."

It didn't go on the mantelpiece with the others though. I looked for it for ages.

She shifts in her seat and turns the radio on. "No. But you can wish him a good birthday from me, if you like." The word 'good' sounds a bit odd, like it doesn't quite fit. The words never quite fit when Mum talks about Dad.

I pack quickly to go to Dad's house. Mum wants Digger to stay at home but I'm absolutely not having that.

"Digger belongs to all of us," I say. "And he stays with me." I'm cross she's asked again. "You know that!" I shout.

She leaves the room and stomps upstairs and runs a bath.

Dad arrives, late and in a right panic.

114

"Kathy ordered all the food but there's been a mistake and they've left out the cheese board so we need to get one. Come on, quick." He grabs Digger's lead and lifts the boot. He doesn't ask about the vet's. Digger seems the last thing on Dad's mind.

I climb in the car and we set off. We drive in silence and then Dad's phone rings.

"Can you see who it is?" he says. I lift his phone.

"It's Gran. She's FaceTiming!" I swipe the screen at the same time Dad says, "Leave it. I'll call her later." But it's too late.

Gran is there, sitting in her white cane chair on her terrace in Spain, the sunshine beaming down.

"Hi, Gran!" I say and I wave hard.

"Hi, James! Happy birthday, Peter, love!" shouts Gran. She always yells on FaceTime, as if no one can really hear her. "Ooh, I can just see Digger in the back!"

I turn round and put the phone nearer to Digger.

"He is the cutest dog!" says Gran.

I don't think Gran knows about Digger being ill. I don't think now is the time to tell her.

"When are you coming over?" I ask. "You've not been back since Christmas."

"Soon, James," she says. "Promise. Now where are you off to?"

"We need to buy cheese," I say. "For the party."

"Your dad hates cheese," says Gran.

"I know," I say.

The supermarket is up ahead.

"I'll call you back later, Mum," says Dad. "In a bit of a rush."

"OK, love," shouts Gran. "But I'll sing now in case you're too busy eating Gorgonzola to call." She sings 'Happy Birthday', really loud.

"Thanks. Bye, Mum!" says Dad.

I do our virtual-hug thing we always do and then say bye.

"Gran's right," I say. "We don't need a cheese board. It's your party and you hate cheese."

"Kathy says every party has to have a cheese board." He says it in a bit of a mimicky voice. I like that. "Did you bring something decent to wear?"

I look down at what I'm wearing.

"I'm fine in this," I say. I'm not even sure I've packed a spare T-shirt.

Dad grips the steering wheel. "James. Kathy has put hours of work into this party. Loads of people are coming. I don't even know half of them. You can't wear an old football jumper and torn jeans."

"Why not?" I say. "I don't want to meet anyone. I thought that was why Tomaz was invited. So me and him can just hide with Digger upstairs."

"I think Kathy wants you to hand round crisps."

"I don't want to."

"You might just have to," says Dad. He pats my knee. "Do it for me."

We find a parking space at the supermarket. Dad winds down the windows for Digger.

"Cheese board and a shirt," says Dad as we walk inside.

He phones Kathy from the cheese aisle. She wants something called Saint Agur. We can't see it. We buy a box of different cheeses. Dad is sweating. We find me a shirt. It's a bit small with a button-down collar. I hate it. It looks like a tablecloth.

We pick up Tomaz on the way back to Kathy's house. He is in a T-shirt and jeans. No rips. Maybe I can get him to wear the new shirt instead.

"How's Digger?" asks Tomaz.

"He's OK," I say.

Digger's head is between us, resting on the back shelf. His nose rustles into Tomaz's hair. Tomaz laughs and twists his hand back to tickle him.

"Did you get the results?"

Dad turns the radio down. He turns his head very slightly as if he is trying to hear.

"Next week." I say it loudly so Dad can hear too. "And then we speak to the special vet and then we make a plan."

"Cool," says Tomaz. "I've brought tons of sweets." He opens his bag to show me. Dad turns up the radio. "Oh, and this is for you, Peter." He holds up a bottle of wine. "Mum and Dad sent it."

"That's so kind, thank you," says Dad.

"Oh," I say, "and Mum says to have a good birthday."

It sounds even odder now I've said the good bit. I should have changed it to happy. Especially as Tomaz's mum sent wine and my mum, who Dad was married to, just sent a 'good'.

"Thanks," says Dad. He shuffles in his seat.

Kathy is waiting by the front door when we arrive. Dad passes her the box of cheese and she stares at it through the plastic cover.

Digger pulls me up the path. Tomaz gets tangled in the lead. He drops his bag and the sweets fall out, packets littering the path. He laughs really hard, which makes Digger run and dive at him until the two of them are rolling around together.

"Ice," says Kathy. "We need ice."

Dad ignores her.

"Look what Tomaz has given me." He shows her the wine. She looks at the label and just one nostril lifts and I am very, very glad Tomaz is having to chase a packet of Rolos down the sloped path and doesn't see.

"Don't do that," says Dad.

"Do what?" says Kathy.

"That thing you do," says Dad. "That judging thing."

"I've worked myself to a pulp," says Kathy, "and that's all you have to say."

She goes inside and Dad stops and stares at the wine, breathing hard.

"I've got a pressie for you," I say.

"Thanks, love. Can I have it later?"

I nod. Tomaz joins us. Then Digger pushes through Dad's legs, asking for a cuddle.

I've been called down to hand round crisps. Digger isn't allowed downstairs. One of Kathy's friends is allergic to dogs. It makes her come out in a rash. So Tomaz is upstairs with Digger. I tried to get him to help instead. I told him he could have the new shirt. But he didn't want it.

Dad's right. He said he didn't know many people coming and I don't think he does. His mate Jonny is here with his wife Suzie. They used to do loads with Mum and Dad. But tonight they are standing by the front window, looking at Kathy's glass sculptures. They give me the creeps. Not Jonny and Suzie. The sculptures with the funny holes in the middle of the glass.

The house looks like a party palace. There are loads of balloons and a big banner that says 'Happy Birthday Dude'. I've never heard Kathy call Dad 'Dude'. The coffee table has been cleared and there is a pile of presents. Bottles in bags and large wrapped gifts. One label says 'From Colin and Jasper'. I've never heard of them. I think about getting my present and adding it to the pile but it would look a bit tiny.

Dad comes in, laughing. He seems much happier. "Hey, mate, great you're here to help."

"Are these all yours?" I ask, pointing at the table.

"Think so," he says, and he hands me the crisps in a big red bowl. "Can you pass them round?"

A man with a beard and a gold chain comes in and wraps his arm around Dad. I wonder if that is Colin or maybe Jasper. I offer him a crisp. He takes one and then leads Dad away. They are talking about golf. I follow them into the kitchen. It's packed. I have to wait to go in, which feels really silly. The adults all squeeze past each other so I do the same, holding the bowl out in front of me.

A lady with hair like candyfloss takes a handful and says, "You must be Peter's little boy."

I want to say, *You must be the candyfloss clown*, but of course I can't. The man with her mutters something and she roars with laughter, her neck thrown back, the candyfloss moving in one large clump. She laughs so hard she spits out little drops all over the crisps. I'm not sure what to do. I have to shuffle past all sorts of people to find the bin for the spitty crisps and then the packet to refill the bowl.

The kitchen counters are covered in plates of food. I've never seen so much. Dad is with Kathy now. She is wearing a tight dress and very high heels. I take the bowl over to them. Dad doesn't see me but Kathy does. She leans over and takes a crisp and says really loudly, "Thanks, love, you're being such a help."

The people standing with them all take one too.

Thanks, love.

She has never called me love.

I do not want to be her love.

Just like I don't want to be Dave's mate.

I lean closer to Dad.

"I haven't given you my present yet."

"OK, OK," says Dad.

Kathy drapes herself back round him, one arm sort of wrapped around his neck as if she could yank at any moment and poor Dad would end up with a cricked neck and have to wear a cone, like Digger.

"I've given him mine," says Kathy. She kisses him. "Show James."

"Later, Kath," says Dad. "Later."

"Why?" she says, pulling back from him a little. "Don't you like it?"

"Of course..."

Dad pulls up his sleeve. He has a huge new watch. It's bright silver.

"What happened to Uncle Bobby's watch?" I say. "You always wear Uncle Bobby's watch."

Kathy turns away to the table and rearranges the mini pasties. Dad stares at me hard, tilts his head slightly as if I'm spoiling things.

"And I will again," says Dad. "But this is my new birthday watch." He pulls Kathy in. "And I love it."

Kathy takes another crisp from the bowl I'm still holding. I wish I'd left the ones with candyfloss spit all over them.

And then there is a crash. I turn round fast. Digger is jumping up at the table, his tongue all over the meats and cheeses.

Kathy shrieks.

Someone yells, "I'm allergic!"

Digger has the main plate of meat on the floor and is stuffing as much roast beef in as he can.

Dad gets him by the collar. Kathy is grabbing at the mini pasties, hooking them out from under the cupboard. One of her high pointy heels stabs one, right in the middle, the

122

pastry flapping like a loose plaster.

Someone yells, "Five-second rule!" There is laughter and then Tomaz appears.

"I just had to go for a quick pee. Sorry."

Candyfloss is picking dog hairs off the salami, lifting each one up to the light to inspect the damage.

I want to laugh. I want to just wrap myself around Digger and collapse in giggles. For a moment I wish Dave was there. He would have enjoyed it.

I get hold of Digger. "I'll take him," I say.

"Yep," says Dad.

We turn to go and I hear Kathy muttering as she picks up the cheese board. It's upside down, with all the cheese flattened underneath.

"Couldn't the dog have just stayed with Jackie? Surely if he's sick, he shouldn't be here anyway."

I look at Dad. He's just standing there, hands on his hips, staring at the floor. Candyfloss wraps an arm round Kathy and leads her away, telling her they will clear up. Dad stares at Kathy's back as she leaves the room. I don't think I have ever seen him look so unhappy.

Tomaz and I take Digger into the front hall. Jonny and Suzie are there, trying to find their coats.

"We're heading off," says Suzie.

"OK," I say.

"Can you wish your dad a happy birthday from us?" says Jonny.

"Yep, I will," I say.

And then Suzie hugs me, like she used to do when I was little, and it takes me back to when Mum and Dad lived together, in my house.

They leave and we go up to my room, shutting the door firmly.

"Sorry about that," says Tomaz. "I know I was meant to keep Digger in."

"Don't worry about it," I say. "It was great."

I'm stroking Digger, my hands smoothing down his coat, picking out the food stuck in his fur. There's a bit of roast beef under his collar, where he can't reach.

"Did you see the cheese?" laughs Tomaz, covering his mouth as if to smother the sound. "It was like a pile of sludge. I think Digger skidded on it."

"So funny!" I say.

"I heard what Kathy said," says Tomaz. "About Digger."

I can't say anything. I can't talk.

Tomaz gets out his phone and taps away. I sit next to him and watch.

"When are you getting yours?" says Tomaz.

"My what?"

"Your new phone," he says. It sends a flash of irritation

through me. My phone is a horrid old brick that runs out of charge in a day and can't do anything. It's for 'emergencies,' which is pointless as I never have it on me.

"When we start high school," I say. "My parents' stupid rule." It seems odd saying parents. As if they are a team. It's about the only thing in two years they've agreed on. The timing of my new phone. One that actually works and does stuff.

Tomaz's fingers whizz over the screen, making the aliens dive.

I don't want Digger to know I'm irritated. I rub his paw and settle him on the rug and he flops down to go to sleep.

"I'll be right back," I say to Tomaz and then I go to the loo and wash my face. When I come out, I peep over the bannisters. There are a few people in the hall, waiting to use the loo by the front door. I go back to my room.

"I've got an idea," I say. I pull out my box of things that I keep at Dad's. There's an old blaster gun there with foam bullets. "Let's take it in turns, see who we can get?"

We sit between the bannisters, looking down at the hall, watching the party people go in and out of the downstairs loo. The music is really loud now. We aim at each loo user but the bullets don't fire very well. Most of them end up on the stairs. When it's quiet, one of us rushes down and collects them. It's quite exciting, that bit.

One man finds a bullet by the front door. He picks it up and looks around. But we have retreated to my room and he just sees Digger's face staring over the railings.

We reload and sit and wait. And then someone appears. I grab Tomaz's arm. He has the gun.

"This one," I say. "Get this one."

Tomaz aims, takes a while before he pulls the plastic trigger. He shoots the foam bullet long and steady. It glides down the stairs and catches Candyfloss, right in her mop of hair. The red foam bullet hangs there. She doesn't even feel it. She goes into the loo and we collapse in fits of laughter on the landing.

After a while, the loo visitors stop coming.

I hear Kathy shrieking that the cake is ready. I wonder if someone will call me. I wonder if I should go down. But then everyone is singing and cheering. And then the music is on again, loud and thumping through the house.

Digger is restless. I realize he hasn't been out for a while and it's getting late. So we get his lead and take him downstairs and out to the front garden. He instantly pees, a long leg-up stream that hits Kathy's stone statue. And then I hold him close because it's very late and Digger barks at shadows in the dark.

I hear voices. On the other side of the hedge, on the pavement, there is a little group huddled under a streetlight.

Candyfloss is there, the orange light bouncing off her hair, the bullet still dangling.

Digger pulls away and starts turning, his tail lifting. I know what's coming. I feel in my pocket for a poo bag.

"I'm tired," whispers Tomaz.

"OK. You go in," I say. "I'll be up in a bit."

While I'm waiting, I catch bits of chat.

"*Do you think it'll last?*"

"*What, Kathy and Peter?*"

"*She wants that ring you know. She keeps hinting.*"

"*Don't think he'll get married again.*"

Dad and Kathy get married? I can't even imagine it. How do these people know what my dad wants? I wonder if Dad knows she wants to get married. My heart races. I'm not sure I want to hear any more. I know I shouldn't be listening. But I can't move. Digger's arched his back and is mid-flow.

"*The last thing she wanted was a kid around.*"

"*And a dog.*"

"*A sick one at that…*"

A few of them laugh. They actually find it funny.

Digger finishes. I shove the bag back in my pocket and leave the pile of poo right there on the grass. We scuttle back inside and up the stairs and I close my bedroom door.

Tomaz is in his sleeping bag, fast asleep.

I settle Digger.

127

I'm breathing fast, judders of breath, in and out.

I'm glad they think Dad won't give Kathy a ring. I'm glad she didn't want a kid around. I don't want to be around. But Digger. It's not Digger's fault he's sick.

I cry a little into his fur, trying hard not to let it show. I check his dressing and feel all over his body for lumps. Nothing. I attach the cone. He lifts one paw, scratching at it.

"Just a few more nights," I say and I hug him tight and reach for my pyjamas. Dad's present is in my bag, his card Sellotaped on top. I take it out and slide it under the bed, right under, so it hits the back wall. And then I get into bed and listen to the front door bang as the guests leave. I'm just drifting off as I hear a shriek from outside and a screech of "Yuck!" and I feel glad.

Saturday 16th June

Digger's nose nudges me. I wake in a tunnel of plastic with a wet tongue on my cheek. I unclip the cone and sit up. Tomaz is stirring.

"It's nine," he says, looking at my clock. He pulls his sleeping bag up around him. "I had Digger on my feet all night."

The house is quiet so we creep downstairs. Tomaz picks up a bullet from the bottom step and puts it in his pocket. Digger races past us and we follow him into the kitchen. I find the back-door key and let him out.

"Wow," says Tomaz, staring at the mess. There are bottles lined up on every counter, plates of half-eaten food. It's odd seeing Kathy's house like this. It's normally so empty and clean. I think I prefer it this way.

I get juice from the fridge and take two plastic cups from a stack by the sink. My foot slips, skids a bit. I've only got socks on. I lift it to look. It's covered in sludge.

"Must have been the cheese," says Tomaz and we both smile, remembering. I peel the socks off and stuff them in my pocket and we go outside. Digger is racing around, sniffing the bushes. He looks so healthy and fit. The bandage doesn't bother him. The leg is fine. The cancer must be gone. It must be.

"Hey, guys." Dad's at the back door. He looks rough, his hair sticking up like straw. Digger runs to him and nudges his leg. "How about you two have brekkie and take Digger to the park and then we'll drop Tomaz home. Might pop to the bike shop after." He goes back into the kitchen.

"Is that OK?" I ask Tomaz.

"Great," he says, sipping his juice. "I brought a football."

I'm glad I have Digger. I don't feel like playing football. Tomaz kicks the ball and heads it, chasing it when he misses. We walk towards the goalposts. And then I don't want to be here at all. Philip is hanging off the side post. He is with Jez and Mikey, two lads from high school. They were in primary with us last year. Philip hangs out with them a lot. Tomaz sees them too. He keeps kicking the ball but he stays closer to me and we walk a bit slower.

Digger wants to explore the bushes at the side of the field.

I let him, the lead stretched out between us. I glance back. Philip has seen us. He's walking over.

Tomaz keeps kicking the ball.

"What's wrong with him?" says Philip.

I jerk my head up. "What do you mean?" I say.

Philip points at Digger's white bandage. "His leg. What's he done?"

I don't want to tell Philip. Tomaz holds the ball still and stares at me.

Digger sees another dog coming and pulls towards it, which is good as I move away and don't have to answer.

Jez and Mikey walk over. Tomaz starts kicking again. But he loses the rhythm and the ball rolls towards Mikey. Mikey taps it with his foot and starts dribbling. He's not very good.

Philip reaches towards Digger. It seems too obvious to pull him back so I let Philip pat him and then he kneels down and strokes his fur.

Mikey and Jez kick the ball to each other. Digger watches, panting. He thinks this is just a fun game. I loosen the lead, pull him, start to walk away. But he won't come. He wants to stay and play the game.

"Give me the ball," says Tomaz, but Mikey just picks it up and stares at him and moves closer, rolling the ball around in his hands.

And then a good thing and a bad thing happens.

Dad walks on to the field, calling our names. I suddenly feel very young, as if he's come to pick us up because we are not allowed out on our own.

"We need to go," shouts Dad. "Tomaz has to get home for a haircut. I forgot."

Digger sees Dad and leaps forwards. The lead gets caught between me and Mikey. It catches the back of Mikey's legs and trips him right over. He is splayed out on the grass, his face in the mud, the ball flung clear. He kneels up, glares at each of us, pushes Philip as if it's his fault.

"Daddy's here," says Mikey in a babyish voice.

"Shut up," I say, and I turn away with Digger and head towards Dad.

Tomaz grabs the ball. "Idiots," he says.

"Yep," I say, and we follow Dad back across the field.

Kathy is sitting on a tandem.

"No way!" says Dad. "I'm not riding one of those."

"Just try it, babe," says Kathy. "This way we can be together."

Kathy doesn't really seem to get it. I can't see the tandem going over roots and into muddy puddles.

The bikes in the shop smell amazing. Shiny metal with

polished rubber seats. The floor squeaks as we walk around.

"What about this one, James?" Dad pulls out a black mountain bike with suspension forks. I gasp at the price, then I hold the label up and show him.

He shrugs a bit. "Don't worry about that," he says. "This is about you and me getting back on our bikes." I think he thought Kathy was still balanced on the tandem. But she is right behind us.

"Great, thanks," she says. "I thought it was meant to be for all of us."

"It is." Dad sighs.

And then she sees the price label. "Have you seen this? As if that's gonna happen." She turns away and marches over to the black sofa in the middle of the shop and picks up a mountain bike magazine and flicks through it as if she really is looking for something.

Dad's looking at the label again.

"It's too much," I say.

"We can pay for it over time," he says. "They do good deals here."

"Is that what 'interest-free credit' means?" I say. He pulls me close.

"Yep. I want us to do this." He lifts his arm free and pushes on the handlebars, watching the forks lift up and down.

"Does it work like Digger's vet insurance?"

Dad stops, lifts the saddle and slides the bike back into the rack.

"Bit like that, yeah," he says. He pushes the bike hard. The chain catches. And then he goes back to Kathy and it seems the bike shopping is over.

I think we need to find a different shop with less fancy bikes.

Dad and Kathy are still clearing up, right into the evening. The recycling bin is already full so Dad asks me to load all the empty bottles into cardboard boxes by the back door. He's going to give me a bit of extra pocket money for helping.

"Did you enjoy it?" he asks.

"What?" I ask.

"The party?"

"Oh, yeah. Course." I don't like lying to Dad.

"I hope Tomaz had fun," says Dad. I think of Tomaz aiming that bullet at Candyfloss.

"Definitely!" I say, laughing.

Dad smiles. "Sorry we didn't buy bikes today," he says.

"That's OK," I say. "We were just getting some ideas."

Dad stops scraping plates and stares at me for a second.

"I'm so proud of you," he says.

Kathy comes in with a carrier bag. "Tomaz left this," she says. "It was under the desk."

"It's fine, it's mine," I say.

Dad comes closer and peers into the bag. "It's your helmet," he says.

"Yeah," I say. "I just brought it in case, you know, we went cycling. But it doesn't matter. It's probably way too small anyway." I pick up two more bottles and take them outside. All the boxes are full so I have to go and find another in the shed. When I come back in, Kathy is on her phone.

"They rent them out," she says. "By the day or week."

"How about cycling in the forest?" says Dad to me. "Tomorrow. It was Kathy's idea."

"You just turn up," says Kathy. She's still tapping away. She wanders out of the kitchen, carrying a bag of rubbish.

"What do you think?" says Dad.

"Great," I say. Dad pulls the helmet out of the bag and puts it on my head.

"New helmet, definitely!" he says, and we both laugh as it hardly fits over my ears.

Sunday 17th June

The forest car park is heaving with cars and people and dogs and bikes. Kathy is scrunched down in her seat, her head buried in the collar of her jacket. She's wearing her workout leggings and she's brought her armband phone holder, the thing she uses when she goes out jogging. But right now it's hard to believe this trip was her idea.

"I could just wait in the café," she says. We stare out of the windows. The drizzle falls gently until we are watching through rain-spattered glass.

Dad's quiet for a moment, as if he's going to agree.

Come on, Dad. Agree.

"We talked about this," he says, squeezing her knee. "This is for all of us."

It seems everything with Dad is now about 'all of us'.

I get out of the car a bit quick and the door bangs on the van parked next to us.

"Careful," snaps Dad and he leaps out and leans over to

check for marks. "It's fine. Come on."

I want to be at home with Digger. He only had a short walk before we came. I just wish we had ditched this idea and brought Digger to the forest instead.

"Let's go home," I say and I get back in the car. Kathy has just got out. She's staring at the sky, her arms wrapped around her tummy.

Dad opens my door and leans in. "Come on, love. Sorry I was a bit snappy. I want to do this. We'll hire some great bikes. It'll give us an idea of what we want to buy."

Kathy walks off towards the visitor centre.

"Look," says Dad. "Kathy's keen."

We are quiet for a moment. We both know that's not true.

"Why didn't she stay at home?" I say. "Why do we *all* have to do this?"

Dad sighs. "She wanted to be with us."

"She wants to be with you, Dad," I say. "Not me."

Dad starts to say something and then stops. I try to close my door but he is holding it tight.

"Why can't you just tell the truth?" I say and then I shuffle across to the other side and climb out.

I follow Dad across the car park and we both stop at the door of the visitor centre. Dad whistles in an impressed kind of way. The forest isn't far from home but we haven't been here for ages. It's completely changed. They have built a new café and a shop, and inside there are large TV screens showing bikers on the trails and riders in the new skateboard park.

Dad looks for Kathy. She is talking to a couple of people. I think I recognize them from the party. She calls Dad over.

"We won't be long," says Dad and he leads me over to them. They all laugh and joke and I feel very small and out of place. I look around the room, at the bikes on the wall and the racks of helmets.

"Maybe see you on the trails," says Kathy to her friends, and they all do this kiss thing and they leave.

"Come on," says Dad. "Let's go and rent some bikes."

"They said they loved the party," says Kathy. "OK, I'm ready for this." She stands with us, looking at a large chalkboard with all the prices. It's funny how much more ready she is, now that she knows her friends are cycling too.

We have to fill in some details on a tablet.

The lady behind the counter looks at me. She has tattoos on her arms and lots of earrings. "Done much cycling?" she asks, smiling.

"A bit," I say.

"Cool. The trails are in great shape. Let's get you all helmets."

She turns to the racks behind her and brings out three helmets. And then Dad stops her and says, "Just two." He looks at me. "We're going to buy you a new one today. Yes?"

I shrug and smile.

"Great," says the lady. "Good idea. They're on the racks over there." She points to the large display. "I'll get your bikes ready while you buy one."

We walk over. There are so many choices. Kathy scans the rack, pulls on a few chinstraps.

"What colour?" says Dad.

"Red," I say. "Of course." He picks one from the bottom rack for me to try. And then Kathy leans over and taps him.

"I'd go a bit higher spec if I were you," and she shows him the information printed on the more expensive helmets. "I think James needs more comfortable padding," and then she walks away and flicks through a rack of hooded tops.

"Right," says Dad. "Absolutely." He turns back to the helmets and looks at me and it's funny because his eyebrows are lifted and so are mine.

My bike is good. It's great. I want to just pedal and pedal and jump and race, but the trails near the visitor centre are easy and busy and it's hard to go fast. So we trundle along, the three of us. The rain stops and we all take off some layers. Dad puts them in his rucksack. We set off again.

139

The path narrows.

Then Kathy starts to complain. Her bike is too big. The track is too bumpy. It's all too difficult. We climb a gentle hill and at the top we have to choose which trail to take. There is a bench so we stop for a drink and Kathy gets off her bike and sits down.

"You go on," she says. "I'll wait here. You can loop back and get me later. Come back for me in about half an hour." She takes her phone out. "Go on. I don't want to do the longer route."

Dad stares at her. He stares at her for quite a while. "Are you sure?" he says.

"Of course."

He gets back on his bike. I get on mine and follow him.

We choose the harder trail, fly across roots and stones and through the grassy patches. We climb up a super-high hill at the back of the forest and look down over the pine trees. We sit on an old tree stump and eat flapjacks. And then we wind our way back through the trees and join the open trail again. We cycle really fast and then after a bit, Dad skids to a halt and I stop beside him. We are both panting. He grabs his water bottle from the frame. And then he leans over to me and grabs me hard and hugs me tight and I hug him back.

Kathy is sitting outside the café, coffee cup in one hand, phone in the other. She is staring at the screen, tapping away. I'm pretty sure she knows we're back but she doesn't lift her head.

"You OK?" says Dad.

It's like the joy has drained out of him. Like his helmet had a little plug labelled 'joy' and when the helmet came off, it all escaped.

Kathy's smiling now and laughing. But only at the phone.

"We went all the way back to the bench for you," Dad says to her. "You could have phoned me, told me you'd come back."

She slurps from her coffee cup. "Are there any trails you *didn't* ride?" she says, glancing at him. "I said come back in half an hour."

"You said, *about* half an hour. We were forty minutes."

She looks at Dad with slanted eyes. "It started raining again," she says. "You've got my jacket. I got cold." She does look a bit pale and wet.

"Come on, James," says Dad. He lifts up Kathy's bike, picks her helmet up off the floor and then wheels both bikes back towards the shop.

I follow. My bike feels heavy now and the chain catches on my leg.

We return everything and go back outside. Kathy is still there, head down. Dad opens the rucksack and gives her the jacket.

"Bit late now," she says but she grabs it and puts it on.

"I'll get the car," says Dad, and he stomps off and I feel pretty sure he wants to be on his own.

I hover away from Kathy and stare at the ice-cream board.

And then I see Philip. And he sees me. He's on a skateboard. He is with Jez and Mikey. Twice in one weekend. How lucky am I? They come towards me.

"Hey, Titch," says Mikey, circling round me on his skateboard. He always calls me Titch. I got away with it yesterday. I smile to myself thinking of him splayed out on the grass.

"What you doing?" says Philip.

"Nothing," I say, glancing at Kathy, checking she's not listening. She's got her head down still.

Mikey spits out his gum. Jez picks up his board and wipes the dirt off the side. Jez never says much. I don't know why he hangs out with Mikey.

"Think he was spending time with Daddy again," says Mikey and then he leans closer. "Nice helmet," he says and he grabs it out of my hand. "Looks brand new."

"OK, let's go," says Philip. He's fidgeting and flicking his hair and looking around him, as if he expects an adult to appear.

Mikey puts the helmet on his head and he sets off again, turning in big circles. The area is a drop zone for cars. It has big white diagonal lines all over it. They aren't meant to be on their skateboards here. I glance back towards the visitor centre, hoping someone will see. But Mikey skates away, into the car park, up and down the driving lanes, sometimes close to the cars. Jez gets his phone out. I watch Mikey closely, almost hoping Dad drives past him and recognizes the helmet. But I can't see Dad's car and when Mikey comes back towards us, he has the strap in his mouth and is chewing on it, looking straight at me, checking I've seen.

Philip rides away on his board.

I've spotted Dad's car now. He's in a queue, winding his way round to the drop zone.

I turn back. Mikey has taken my helmet off. He is talking to someone. And then my stomach is in my mouth and the flapjack I ate just half an hour ago is making its way back up.

Mikey is talking to Kathy. She is pointing at him, her words flying out fast and hard.

Mikey turns to look at me. His cheeks are red and his eyes are wide. I'm not sure what to do. So I shrug. I don't know why. It just happens. Like I'm with him on this one. Which I'm obviously not.

Kathy puts her hand out for the helmet but at that moment a black truck loaded with bikes pulls in to the drop zone. The driver beeps the horn and waves at them to move on. They split, making way for the truck and Mikey takes his chance to skateboard away, the helmet dangling from his wrist by the strap. He joins Jez and then I spot Philip, up ahead, at the entrance, waiting for them. Kathy sets off towards them. I shout after her.

"Don't."

She spins round to face me. My breath is fast, my mouth bone dry.

"Why?" she says. "Little wretches aren't getting away with that. We need to get it back."

"I know them," I say. "One of them's in my class. They're just messing around. I'll get the helmet tomorrow." I have no idea how I'll manage that, but I don't want Kathy getting involved.

She walks back towards me.

"OK. If you're sure?"

I nod, hard.

"He's a charmer, the one who took the helmet, isn't he?" She looks at me and I look at her. She has freckles on her nose.

"They're idiots," I say.

"I can tell," she says. I look away and shuffle my feet and for one horrid moment I think I'm going to cry. "I want to know," she says, "if you don't get it back, OK?"

I nod again but I can't say anything else.

"I'm going to the loo. Won't be long." And she walks away, her arms folded tight.

I look for the boys. I just spot them, near the entrance to the car park. Philip looks annoyed. He's shouting a bit with his hands raised. Mikey takes my helmet and chucks it high and far, over the fence. And then the three of them skate away, fast.

Dad pulls up. "Where is she *now?*" he says, looking around for Kathy.

I climb in. "The loo."

"Oh, for goodness' sake."

I want to say something but I can't decide what. It's like the words are queued on my tongue. '*She helped me,*' sounds really odd and I don't want Dad knowing about the helmet. '*She's been all right,*' would be even odder. Why would I suddenly say that?

The car behind beeps at us to move on. Dad says a bad word. He has to pull over and park up and lose his place in the queue while we wait for Kathy.

"Honestly," he says. "I've just about had enough for one day."

I sit back and look outside. The fun on the bikes seems ages ago now. Dad's phone beeps. He looks at the text and says another rude word.

"You OK?" I ask.

"Just some idiot. He's been messing me around for weeks. I've had loads of offers for this car but I kept it for him…" He taps away and I know he won't hear anything else I say. I look at the shop and the cyclists and their dogs. There is a golden one like Digger. I want to get home and take him to the park.

After a few minutes, Kathy gets in. Dad rejoins the queue of crawling cars. As we reach the exit gate I look over to the left and past the fence and I can just see my helmet, its red plastic top poking out of the grass.

I'm lying on my bed. Digger is right beside me, curled in a ball. I'm worried about the helmet. Dad's not said anything yet. He hasn't noticed it's gone. And now me and Kathy share this thing, about the boys taking it. I hate secrets. Secrets live under your skin and find their way into every part of you.

They call it my room but it's not *really* my room. Kathy's work desk is in the corner. She uses the room to run her mobile nail business. There are shelves covered in little coloured bottles. Files, cotton wool. It's all here. There are some faded photos on the wall of her with 'famous clients'. She showed them to me when I first stayed over. One is of a singer who got through to the second round of that show with the golden buzzer and the second is of a lady from TV who played the fairy godmother in a panto in town. "I saw that panto," I'd said. "With Mum. It wasn't very good." Kathy stopped showing me the photos then.

I have a bed, a small chest of drawers and a box with stuff like Lego and the blaster guns. Before the party, I hadn't opened the box for ages. It's like a part of me frozen in time. James, aged nine, the James that existed when Dad first moved to Kathy's house.

The bedding is covered in Spider-man. There is a rug in the shape of a Tyrannosaurus rex. My old dressing gown is hanging on the door hook. Too small for me now. And yet it still hangs there. It's like I'm growing up and nothing in this room has noticed. Maybe I'll be at college and when I come to Kathy's house my room will be just the same, as if nine-year-old James still stays here.

I can just see the blue smear on the door behind the dressing gown. It's a nail-polish stain and all around it are scratch marks where I tried to rub it off. There is another smear on the carpet under the bed. That one's got lots of tufts yanked out around it where I tried to get the polish out.

Coming soon ... to a big screen near you... James, aged nine, helpless, alone, desperate ... took on the beast that is ... duh, duh, duhhhh ... blue nail polish...

It had been my second time ever staying at Kathy's house. Dad and I were setting up the room. We had moved the furniture around a bit. I wanted my bed against the long wall. We had to move the desk so we put the bottles of nail polish in a box. Kathy had come up with drinks and biscuits but when she saw all her things in the box, she had left the room really quickly and I heard her stomp downstairs. Dad went to find her. I didn't see him again for hours. I had unpacked my things and then lined Kathy's bottles back on the work desk where they were before. I thought I should try and make things easy for Dad. But when he didn't come back and I was there for ages, doing it all on my own, that's when I opened the bottle of blue polish. A smear on the back of the door and one on the carpet. The stuff stuck like glue. I didn't know it would be like that. I thought it would clean off. I worried for months about that polish. I still don't know if Dad or Kathy have ever seen my two blue smears of misery.

There is a knock on the door. I sit up a little.

"James," says Dad. "I've brought you some birthday cake."

He opens the door and hands me a plate. "You didn't have any on Friday, did you?"

I shake my head.

"I'm not hungry," I say and I place it on the bed.

Dad moves it on to Kathy's desk and sits down next to me. He reaches for Digger and strokes the golden dome on his head. "I remembered your present. I didn't open it. Where is it?" I shrug. "James, please. I feel awful. Your present is the most important of any. Please."

I shrug again. I really don't want to give it to him right now. It's like it's yesterday's thing. I think it's still under the bed, up against the wall, probably next to the blue smear.

I walk over to the desk and pick crumbs off the slice of cake. A few drop on to a shiny paper flyer for Kathy's business. There is a photo of her on the front. One crumb is on her cheek, like an extra freckle.

"OK," says Dad. He pats his knees and stands up. "Not much more I can say." Digger jumps off the bed.

"I enjoyed the bike ride," I say, picking at the icing.

He opens the door. "Good," he says. "So did I."

Digger follows him.

"I'll come now," I say. "Digger needs his tea."

They go downstairs and I eat a bit of cake and it tastes stale.

Monday 18th June

Philip is by the school gate, kicking it with his foot, the metal banging hard against the frame. I walk past him, head down. And then he is beside me and he shoves a carrier bag against my tummy.

"Here," he says. "I got it off Mikey."

We walk across the playground, me and Philip, as if we are mates.

I look inside the bag. My helmet.

"He gave it to you, did he?" I ask.

"I made him," says Philip. He kicks a stone across the tarmac. It bounces off a wall.

I want to say, *That's odd because I last saw it sitting in the field at the forest.* But I don't. Because I realize Philip went back to get it. He probably skateboarded home and then went out again, on his own, and climbed over the fence to get it back.

"Thanks," I say.

He shrugs and flicks his hair and walks round the corner on to the field. I think that's as much nice as Philip can take.

I look at the helmet. I don't want to touch the strap. It's been in Mikey's mouth. But at least I have it back. I fold the top of the bag over and then put it into my school bag. And then Tomaz runs over, shrieking about a level he's made on the game he loves. He's been trying to get there for months. So I hear every detail and it's good to just walk and listen.

Mr Froggatt asks about our weekends.

The usual replies come back. Swimming, football, hockey, gaming, shopping. Mr Froggatt likes to hear about our lives. And he tells us about his.

"I bought a wardrobe," he says. "Well, I say a wardrobe. It had three hundred and sixty-two pieces and I couldn't build it and it now has three hundred and seventy-six pieces."

"How does it have more than you started with?" asks Tomaz.

"Because I thought to make it work, I'd cut some bits up but it seems you're not meant to do that."

He tells us how he laid it out like a jigsaw on the lounge carpet.

"And you know what?"

"What?" says India.

"I managed to build it. I managed to get all the parts to kind of fit. But guess what the problem was then?"

"It fell apart?" says Margo.

"Nope," says Mr Froggatt. "I'd glued it too much. With superglue. Nothing fell apart."

"You couldn't get it through the door," says Eva.

Everyone laughs.

"That's right! I couldn't get it through the door," says Mr Froggatt. "And I couldn't unscrew it because I'd glued it."

"So what did you do?" asks Flo.

"Well, Flo, I nearly cried. And then I thought, it's just a wardrobe. And I got a saw and sawed through the bits that were glued and tried to rebuild it upstairs." We all laugh. Even Philip.

"What did you do this weekend, Tomaz?" asks Mr Froggatt.

"I went to a party on Friday night. James's dad's party. And we used blaster guns to shoot at the guests. I got one, didn't I, James?" He spins round to look at me.

"He did," I say.

"Sounds like a good party," says Mr Froggatt.

I nod and smile and I'm glad when India puts up her hand to talk about scout camp.

The bell goes. India is on full detail re-tell. We know the

colour of the rope and how much rain the Lake District has seen in the last ten weeks and how high the river was, higher than any human has ever seen it.

"We'll have to wrap it up there," says Mr Froggatt. "Poetry books are out for any takers. Remember, I can always put new ideas in if you don't like the current suggestion."

We all get up and gather our things. I take my poetry book and I slip it into my bag. Jack is next to me.

Mr Froggatt comes over, checking windows and turning the plant round to face the sun.

"I've not done one yet," says Jack.

"Have a go," says Mr Froggatt.

"But the first one is about a house and I don't want to do that one," says Jack.

Mr Froggatt gets out a pen. "Is there one you do like the idea of?" he asks.

"Insects," says Jack.

And Mr Froggatt writes in Jack's book.

"Can't wait to read it," he says. And then he turns back to the plant and feels the soil to see if it needs water.

Mum's made my favourite chocolate-chip cookies. I take one and slump on to the comfy chair in the kitchen.

Digger rests his head on my knee.

"Your stuff's very muddy," she says, pulling my clothes out from the bag. She takes them to the sink and starts to rinse the worst off.

"Dad said to say sorry he didn't get them washed."

"Oh," says Mum.

"We ran out of time."

"Oh," says Mum.

I take another cookie.

"The mud's from the forest. We hired bikes." I don't say anything else. There's so much I could say. About the helmet and Mikey and Kathy helping but I don't say anything. I pick out a giant chocolate chip and let it sit on my tongue.

"That's nice," says Mum. She squeezes out the socks and shorts and loads them into the machine. "How was the party?"

"Fine," I say.

"Did Gran come over for it?"

"No," I say.

"Anyone I know there?" she says, tipping out my bag.

"Jonny and Suzie," I say, and then I wish I hadn't said it.

Mum lays the bag flat on the table and folds it which is an odd thing to do with the bag as it's big and made of tough material.

"Oh," she says.

"They didn't stay long," I say.

"Oh."

"I'm not sure they had a very good time." And then I feel bad for saying that, as if the party was rubbish. "Everyone else stayed really late though. They drank a lot."

"Oh," says Mum. "That's nice." She scoops some washing powder into the machine and turns the dials. "Hot wash, I think," and she passes me the plate of cookies.

"I've had two," I say.

"One more won't harm you," she says.

Dave walks into the kitchen. "Right, I'm off." He is wearing a shirt and tie and some really bad aftershave.

"Ooh, bit strong," says Mum, wafting a hand in the air. Dave smiles and kisses her.

"Not sure what time I'll be back," he says.

"OK," says Mum. "Good luck with the new client."

Dave nods and pats Digger. It feels a bit odd, Dave going out in the evening in a shirt.

"Dave has to see some new clients, James," says Mum, as if I'm desperate to know where he is going. "They want him looking smart."

Who's he plumbing for now? The queen?

They walk into the hall. Digger follows them. I hear Mum tell Dave she doesn't want him to go. And then he tells her not to wait up. And then he goes. And I'm glad.

Digger comes back into the kitchen with her.

"You're getting him checked tomorrow, yes?" I ask.

"Yes," says Mum. "Charlie's only there in the morning so I'll take him first thing. The results may be in from Friday's tests." She leans down to snuggle Digger and bury her face in him.

"You OK?" I say.

"Yes, fine," she says. "Be a bit quiet without Dave tonight."

I pat Digger and I want to say, *Well, we were OK before Dave came along,* but I don't. I stuff the rest of the cookie in my mouth and I go to my room. Digger follows.

I flop on the bed and pull out the poetry book to see what Mr Froggatt has written.

AN IMPORTANT PERSON

I grew up with my gran
She was my mum, my dad, my biggest fan
She is the most important person to me
And now if you'd like, it would be great to see
If you can write a few lines about a person important to you
Could be Mum, Dad, Uncle or Great-Aunty Lu.

I'm not in the mood to think about people.

DIGGER

People can fight and talk and shout
Digger lifts a paw and asks to go out
People can judge you and make you eat fish
• Digger just gobbles up what's in his dish
People can argue and not like you at all
Digger just wants you to throw his big ball
Whatever you've done, if you whinge or you whine
Digger is there, the same every time
He's the heart of the home, my best hairy friend
I'll love him forever, to the last very end.

Tuesday 19th June

Mum's driving us to swimming this week. She passes us juice cartons and a biscuit each.

"How's Digger?" I ask.

"He got full marks," says Mum. "Charlie is really pleased with how everything has healed. The lymph nodes were clear, James. That's really good news. We should get a call to see the specialist vet very soon. Her name is Fiona. Apparently, she's the best cancer vet in the north west."

I nod.

"Did Charlie say that?" I ask.

"Yes," says Mum.

"Good," I say. I trust Charlie.

"What will Digger need?" says Tomaz.

"We're not sure yet," says Mum. "But it's just to check all the cancer has gone."

We sit back and nibble on our biscuits. I hate the word cancer. We pass the big pub on the corner, the one with the play area with the red dinosaur. The rude words are still there.

"That's one big dinosaur," says Tomaz. "Is it a T. rex?"

I shrug.

"Nice place, that," says Mum. The car stops at traffic lights and she looks over at the pub. I wonder if she is thinking about Dad and the tough meat.

Tomaz passes me his biscuit. The snack quality does not meet his normal standards.

"I hope the pool is clean today," says Tomaz.

I smile at him and he makes a fart sound.

Wednesday 20th June

Dad's car has broken down. He phones to say he can't pick me up and asks if Mum can give me a lift to his house.

"I don't understand," I say. "How can your car break down? You *sell* cars."

"I know, James," he says. "But the starter motor's gone. Kathy's out at work. I'm not sure what time she's home but I can use her car to take you back in the morning."

I ask Mum if she can drop me but she is going out with Gena. She is wearing heels. Mum never wears heels.

"I'll drop you both," says Dave. "On my way to work."

Dave has his shirt on again.

"Are you sure, love?" says Mum.

"A hundred per cent," says Dave.

"So kind of Gena," says Mum, "to buy me a birthday treat like this."

"Your birthday was months ago," I say.

"Which makes it even more special to go out tonight," says Mum.

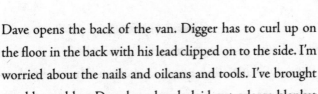

Dave opens the back of the van. Digger has to curl up on the floor in the back with his lead clipped on to the side. I'm worried about the nails and oilcans and tools. I've brought an old towel but Dave has already laid out a large blanket and the van is swept and clean. I lay the towel on top and then get into the van. I want to say thanks for the blanket but the words don't come.

We drop Mum first. She kisses Dave, which makes me retch, and then she joins Gena outside the restaurant. Gena has a very bright orange-and-white dress on.

"Blimey," says Dave. "She looks like a giant traffic cone. At least they won't get run over."

I really want to laugh. A small snort leaks out. We set off, me, Dave and Digger.

"She might stop cars in that dress," says Dave. "Imagine that. A whole pile-up because of Gena." And then he does an impersonation of the police arriving at the scene.

"So what, sir, made you crash into the car in front?"

"Well, gov, a giant cone suddenly appeared from nowhere. Honest! Didn't see a thing, gov. Nothing and then

there it was, floating across the street."

Digger sits up again and paws at the seats.

"Nearly there," I say and I twist round to stroke him, trying to cover up my giggles as I do so.

We pull up at Kathy's house. Dad comes down the path to meet us. I jump out.

"Thanks, Dave," says Dad.

Dave nods and says, "No problem." He points at Dad's car. "Pain, eh?"

"Yeah," says Dad. "Real pain."

Then Dad and Dave talk about starter motors. This is very strange. So I go to the back of the van and open the door. Digger is excited. He's heard Dad's voice. His tail wags madly and he scuffs into the side of the van and then jumps out. I leave the old towel on the blanket, just so Dave knows I had it all sorted.

"See you tomorrow, James," says Dave. He waves and pulls away.

Digger has a spot of grease on his fur. I show Dad and he gets a tissue out of his pocket and tries to wipe Digger's back but it won't come out. He says a bad word.

"Don't let Kathy see," he says. "She's just got back."

He takes Digger's lead and we go inside.

Kathy is sitting on a bar stool in the kitchen, waving her hands. Her nails are deep purple. A row of polish bottles are lined up in front of her.

"I'm trying a new range," she says.

I think I'm meant to say something but I don't know what. So I just nod. She beams at Dad.

"The quality is outstanding," she says and Dad peers over to look.

Digger is pleased to see her. I don't like it when he does this. He wags his tail and goes over for a pat.

"Not now, Digger," she says. He lifts the bad paw and rests it on her leg. She twists away from him, moves her knee to guide him. "Peter, take him, please."

Dad grabs Digger's collar. I pick up the lead. It gets caught on the kitchen stool. I unwind it and feel a little rush of joy. Kathy has white jeans on. With a little streak of grease down the leg that tried to steer Digger away.

"I'll take Digger outside," says Dad, so I pass him the lead.

Kathy blows on her fingernails and watches them leave. I'm about to follow when she says, "James."

I turn back. I think she's seen the grease.

"Did you get the helmet back?"

I nod.

"Good. I'm glad," she says.

I glance at the grease and it looks so much worse than before.

Thursday 21st June

Mum is scraping the bottom of the saucepan.

"Burned it again," she shouts and she bangs the pan into the sink. She whisks up three new eggs and puts bread in the toaster. "It's not a very exciting tea," she says. "Sorry, love."

I'm fiddling with a candle that's burnt out in the holder. It's fun, picking at the dried wax.

Dave appears. He's wearing a new tie. It's shiny red with swirls.

"Do you take the tie off to do plumbing?" I ask. "Or do you just cover up with overalls?"

Dave laughs and goes to ruffle my hair. I duck my head. His laughter stops as if I've punched it away.

"Bit of both," he says. "Bit of both."

I pick at the wax again. Mum stares at the pan and stirs the eggs.

"Won't have to do this forever," says Dave and he kisses her and she nods.

"You should sell cars," I say. "Like Dad." I flick a big chunk of wax and it flies across the table. "Then you wouldn't have to work so late for fussy new clients."

Mum whips round and stares at me. I can feel her desperate to let rip at me. I sniff and chip away at the candle.

"Come on, love," Dave says to Mum, and she follows him out to the hall.

I can hear them whispering. I dig deep into the wax. The pan sizzles and then the room is full of the smell of burning again and I look up and smoke is coming from the toaster.

Friday 22nd June

Mr Froggatt is ill so we have a Miss Brown today. She is about as boring as her name. Her clothes are brown, her shoes are brown. She writes her name on the board and even her writing is boring. She talks in the same tone. No ups or downs in Miss Brown's voice. She has given us pages and pages of sums.

"They start easy and get harder and harder," she says as she hands out the stapled sheets.

"Has Mr Froggatt done a runner?" says Philip.

We all look at Miss Brown for the answer. Maybe Philip is right. Mr Froggatt has moved on. Like the others. The thought makes my tummy hurt.

"He has a touch of flu," says Miss Brown. "He should be back on Monday." She is back at her desk. "Right, you can start," she says but then she picks up a pile of slips. "Actually, one more thing. Mr Froggatt has asked me to confirm who is attending the high-school welcome evening on Monday. A few of you haven't returned slips. India, are you going?"

We all turn round to look at India. Miss Brown walks across the room.

"Where are you, India?" she asks.

"Here," says India. "Um, I think so but I'm super nervous. Apparently the toilets are really clogged. What happens if I need the toilet?"

India is nibbling her fingers and her maths sheet has fallen on the floor. Miss Brown picks it up and puts it back on her desk.

"Maybe use the bathroom before you go, dear," she says. "And don't drink for an hour before."

There are a few sniggers. India smiles and nods and reaches for her pencil and writes her name on the sheet.

"Philip," says Miss Brown. "Are you going? Where are you?"

Philip flips his hand up and shrugs and bends the staple at the top of his sheet. "Do you have any concerns, Philip?" she asks.

"Not about the toilet, miss. I'll be fine." We all laugh and Philip smiles, actually smiles. He shifts forwards, leans back again, pulls a hand through his hair. Smiles again. It's odd that the boring Miss Brown has managed to get Philip to smile. And then he says, "I always do my number two first thing in the morning."

The people that hear what he says laugh again. The ones that didn't whisper, "What did he say? Was that about a number two?"

Miss Brown raises one hand and we are quiet. She stares at Philip for a few seconds and then goes back to her desk. "Work now," she says.

Flo puts her hand up but Miss Brown makes a snappy 'no' signal. I think Miss Brown has been doing this teaching thing a long time.

We work. But the quiet doesn't last. The sums are really hard. Miss Brown expected us to be a bit cleverer than we are. Margo is the only one to finish the little pack of sheets. I gave up on page two. Miss Brown goes through some of the sums on the board. Flo puts her hand up again.

"Mr Froggatt said that long division was invented to give humans one enormous headache."

"He did say that," says India, plonking her pencil down. "And it's so true."

Miss Brown smiles and wipes the board clean. "We have a bit of time left until break," she says. "What's this then?" She picks up the box with the poetry book slit. She sees the note on the front. *Friday – Sharing Day*. She lifts the lid and takes out the books. The room has gone very quiet. It's like Miss Brown is stealing.

"We only say if we want to share," says India, but Miss

Brown doesn't hear. India is nibbling again. Her book is there, in Miss Brown's hands, second in the pile. It has little heart stickers all over it. I've given mine in and there are two others.

"Flo," says Miss Brown, reading the name label on the first book. She looks around for Flo to raise her hand. When Miss Brown starts reading, Flo looks happy. I think Flo agreed to share. But this still all feels wrong.

MY DAD
He's big and fat and smokes a lot
He manages builders on the building plot
He likes football and beer and old postcards
Loving my dad is not very hard
He buys me things and he cooks good food
My dad is great, if he's in a good mood.

"Well done," says Miss Brown. "Remember if you use 'buy' to mean paying for something it's not spelled B-Y-E. There is a 'u' in the middle." She takes off her reading glasses and writes 'buy' on the whiteboard. "And maybe you could use a few more describing words. You used 'good' twice. Maybe you could put 'tasty food' or 'happy mood.'"

Flo is staring at Miss Brown. She nods a little as if she thinks she is meant to. Miss Brown reaches for a red pen and puts a big tick on the page and writes a comment. A flash of something goes round the room. It's not a gasp or a yell. There is no sound. There are shuffled feet and upright bodies and wide eyes but no noise.

And yet we all know.

This is wrong.

Miss Brown has broken the rules.

I want to get my book back. I sit up and stare at the other three books, search frantically for the ripped bit on the edge of mine, hoping it is at the bottom of the pile.

India's book is next.

"Um, miss," mutters India. "I didn't really want to share today..." But Miss Brown is flicking through to find the right page. She isn't listening. She puts her glasses back on and starts to read.

MY SISTER
She's eight this year
With blond curls
She stamps her feet when she's cross
She follows me everywhere
Into the garden, down the stairs
Her little pink coat hangs on a peg
She copies me
And hugs me tight

Every night
In the moonlight.
Or she would,
If she could
My sister,
She's not here
But Mum says she is with me, around me
Just a month old when she died
I cried and cried
But she's with me, Mum says,
And my mum never lies.

Miss Brown closes the book. The room is very quiet. You can hear the water in the tap next door and voices round the classroom sink.

"Oh…" says Miss Brown.

I glance over at Tomaz. He looks back with a puzzled expression.

"How sad," says Miss Brown. "India, where are you?" She looks around the room. She has forgotten that India was the scared toilet girl. Margo has reached out for her and has one arm wrapped around her. India raises her hand a little. There is one single tear on her face. And then the bell rings out for break. It sounds so much louder than normal.

"That's a very special poem," says Miss Brown.

India nods. "I didn't really want it read out. We write 'share' at the top if we want to share. Sorry."

It's funny how India says she is sorry. India followed the rules. Miss Brown should be sorry.

"What was her name?" says Miss Brown.

The room is still very quiet but all around us the school has exploded into break. A football bounces off the window. Children yell down the corridor.

India sniffs a little and says, "Sophie. Her name was Sophie."

"Well, India," says Miss Brown, standing up straight and closing the poetry book. "I think Sophie would absolutely love her poem. I expect she was very beautiful."

India smiles. "She was," she says.

"Would you like to go to break first, India? Choose a friend to take?"

India nods. She wipes her tear away and clutches Margo to her and they scuttle outside.

"I knew about that," whispers Eva.

"So sad," comes another voice.

Miss Brown picks up a few pens and brushes her skirt down and cleans her glasses with a little cloth. We file out of the room. I pass Mr Froggatt's desk and when Miss Brown is fetching her bag, I snatch up my book and take it with me. I wanted to share Digger. But not any more.

Saturday 23rd June

Digger is lying in the sunshine, chewing his fake bone. I lie next to him on the grass. He lifts his paw on to my shoulder. It's the bad paw but things are looking good. The bandage is off now. The fur is starting to grow back, little lines of golden hair popping up over the shaved patch. I run my hand over the scar. He doesn't mind.

My bag is next to me, ready to go to Tomaz's house. I don't want to leave Digger. I'm not really in the mood for a sleepover tonight but we planned it weeks ago.

Dave is digging up one of the borders in the back garden. His jeans are slipping as he works, the waistband going further and further down.

"Pull 'em up!" says Mum. He spins round to look at her. She signals to pull up his waistband. "We don't want to see any more," she says, smiling. Dave tugs them up and carries on.

"Why is he digging up that bush?" I ask.

"It's a weed, James. We're trying to tidy the garden a bit."

Digger runs to join Dave. He stops and pats him and strokes his ears.

"It's got flowers on it," I say.

"It's a weed."

"That plant's always been there," I say.

Digger puts his head in the newly turned soil and wags his tail.

"It's a weed," she says. "And it's going. We're going to tidy up the bushes, trim the tree and try to fix that banging fence panel."

"It's always banged," I say. "And the tree is perfect as it is."

"It just needs a trim to keep it healthy," says Mum. "Like a haircut. Makes the tree grow stronger."

"I'll be very careful, James," says Dave. He takes a rest, leans on his spade, rubs Digger's head.

I walk over to the fence and push it gently. It makes a quiet tapping sound. Uncle Bobby used this fence panel to teach me how to save goals. If I missed the ball it hit the panel. Less than ten bangs and I got sweets.

I call Digger over. I only have a short time with him. Dave has all evening. But Digger doesn't want to come. He wants to dig. And then the doorbell rings.

"Tomaz is here," says Mum. "Come on."

I pick up Digger's bone and take it to him. I put it on the

open soil and then I hug Digger and leave.

"Have fun," says Dave. But I don't turn back.

Tomaz is at the front door with his mum.

"We will bring James back eleven tomorrow, if OK," says his mum.

"Oh gosh, whenever," says Mum and she gives me a hug.

"The garden looking lovely, Jackie," says Tomaz's mum. "You've worked hard." She looks at the pots and the row of lavender.

"Oh, that's kind," says Mum. She leans down to pull up a weed. "It's been a learning curve."

I want to say, *When Dad left Mum, Gena bought so many lavender bushes we couldn't plant them all. She said that the soil would be good for Mum's soul. And then Mum couldn't stop gardening. And now Dave is in the back garden, digging everything up and changing everything and fixing things that don't need fixing.*

But of course I don't say that.

Tomaz holds up a big bag of sweets.

"I made level twelve," he says.

"You never did," I say. We walk down the path together. We put my bag in the boot. Tomaz jumps in the front seat and his mum climbs in and starts the engine.

I walk slowly round to the side door and turn to Mum. She is watching me.

"Don't mend the panel," I say. "It's always banged."

"Have fun," she says, "and try to get some sleep," and then she waves and closes the door and I turn to get in the car.

We eat the best food. Tomaz's mum says it is called pierogi. It's a bit like dumplings but better. I have extra. There is a pudding with pastry and icing. And then we go to the den. It's this big room that Tomaz has just for him. I love being in the den. There are boxes of Lego and a giant screen where we sit and game. Tomaz's sister Anna waddles in and out. She's covered in white icing and Tomaz shouts at her a bit when she touches the control. She is sticky all over. Later she waddles in when she's had her bath and she's in a pink onesie and Tomaz lets her sit on his lap, nestled into him. She watches us while we build a forest landscape, her thumb planted in her mouth. I'd like a sister or a brother. But I have Digger.

We play the game for hours and then we head upstairs. Tomaz has bunk beds. He sleeps in both bits. It depends how he's feeling.

"Which one do you want?" he asks. Last time Jack bagged the top and I had to go on the floor. I point up top and climb the ladder.

"You want some sweets?" asks Tomaz.

"Yeah, OK," I say and he throws me the bag. It spills everywhere.

"We need a pulley thing," I say.

"That would be so cool!" says Tomaz.

We empty Lego from a red bucket and Tomaz goes down to his garage and comes back with a length of stripey rope. We rig it up, pushing the rope through the struts of the bed. We even find some little battery lights to put in the bucket. We turn the main lights off and test it all out. It tips a bit but it works.

We eat a lot of sweets. Tomaz's dad calls out that they are going to bed. We talk for a bit longer and then Tomaz stops talking and his breath is deep and even and I know he is asleep. I lie back and pull the duvet cover free from the duvet and shine the lights from the bucket through the material. It's a bit like my curtains at home. I shut my eyes and listen to the different sounds of Tomaz's house. The pub emptying across the street. The bathroom next door, the toilet filling up after someone's flushed. A distant bark. A voice calling to a dog. And then I turn the little lights off in the bucket and lie back and I miss Digger so much that my tummy feels a bit funny.

Sunday 24th June

The rain pounds down on Tomaz's dad's van. I'm starving. I was too tired to eat breakfast and I feel a bit sick.

"Thanks for coming," says Tomaz's dad as I get out of the van.

"Thanks for having me," I say.

"See you tomorrow," says Tomaz.

I nod and yank my bag out and dash up the path. My trainers splash in the puddles. I ring the bell and knock on the door. Over and over. At last Mum opens it. Her hair is wet from the shower.

"Hey, love," she says. "How you doing?" She lifts a hand to wave at Tomaz's dad. The van pulls away.

Digger runs towards me, wagging his tail.

"He needs to go out," says Mum.

I dump my things and find the key for the back door and let him out. He races to the first bush and lifts his leg. I stand in the doorway and look at the garden.

Bushes have been ripped out and new ones planted. The ivy from the back wall has been scraped away. There is a big pile of garden waste in the middle.

"Thought we might have a bonfire," says Mum.

I walk outside. Digger rolls on the lawn, scratching his back on the damp grass. The tree has been trimmed. The long branch I used to sit on is now half its length.

"It looks awful," I say.

"What?" asks Mum.

"The tree. Why have you trimmed it like that?"

"It needed it, James. I told you that."

"It's not even the right time to trim a tree. We talked about it at school."

"I'm going to dry my hair," says Mum. She closes the door.

I kick the pile of garden rubbish. And then I get my ball and kick it against the panel. It bounces back. No bang. Just a soft click. I go up to the panel and kick it. Nothing. And then I can see Dave has put little wooden blocks in between the post and the panel so I pull them out. All of them. I put them at the bottom of the garden waste pile, tuck them in so no one can see. And then I get my ball and kick it and it bangs again and I do it over and over until I can't kick it any more and I am soaked to the skin.

Digger joins me. He sits quietly by my side. He knows

I'm upset. I stroke his head and we go in. The kitchen is warm and cosy. The radio is on. I have a bowl of cereal and a drink. I go upstairs and find dry clothes. Then I go back down and snuggle into the sofa with Digger, pull the big furry blanket over us. I get the remote control and try to find my favourite programme. The channels are all mixed up and I can't find the TV guide bit.

Mum comes in.

"This stupid thing Dave bought is so confusing," I say. "Where is he?"

"At work," says Mum.

"I can't use the new remote," I say. I sit up and raise my voice and Digger jumps down. "Why did you let him change everything?"

Mum takes the control and has a go. She presses buttons and turns the TV on and off. Digger pads out of the room.

"Why's he at work *again?*" I say. I can't help it. "I thought he wanted to go bowling? Not that I'd want to go bowling with him anyway."

Mum stares at me. She looks like she's going to cry. She presses the button on the side of the TV. The screen goes black. "Go to your room," she says.

I throw the blanket off me and I turn and yell, "Why couldn't everything just stay the same? I want everything to be normal again."

I fly out of the room and pound upstairs. I want to slam my bedroom door but then I hear Digger coming up behind me. So I stop and wait for him and breathe hard. I close the door behind him and hug him and realize that even though Digger is soaking wet, Mum still let him follow me up.

Monday 25th June

Mr Froggatt is back. He's right by the door as we all come in. He pulls India over and talks to her. She nods a lot and smiles. We read for a bit and then Mr Froggatt stops us. He checks over the list for the high-school evening.

"Seems most of you are going tonight," he says. "Good stuff. Ask questions. Look keen. Don't steal anything."

"I would *never* do that," says India.

"It was a joke, India," says Mr Froggatt.

"Oh," says India.

"I might steal some toilet paper," says Philip.

"Only if you've used it," says Mr Froggatt.

"Yuck!" says India.

Mr Froggatt walks round and sits on his desk.

"I am so sorry," he says. "Miss Brown had no idea how the poetry box works. She left me a note. I should have told her. I feel I've let you all down." He picks up the poetry box and lifts the lid, checking inside.

"You better, sir?" asks Jack.

"I am," he says. "But I'm sorry about Friday. Especially to Flo and India."

"It doesn't matter, sir," says Flo.

India agrees, nodding a lot and winding her curls round her fingers.

"She wasn't as nice as you, sir," says Eva.

Mr Froggatt carefully puts the lid back on the box and smiles. "Very nice of you, Eva, but she was only here a day. On her second day of supply, Miss Brown is known for taking the class to the theme park. As many roller coasters as they want."

"Wicked," says Jack.

"As if," says Philip.

"Thank goodness you're better," says India. "Those rides make me really, really sick." And then she winces. Her curls are wound so tight round her fingers that the whole lot is a tangled mess. "I can't feel my fingers!" she says. Margo pulls and yanks and India shrieks and Mr Froggatt goes to help and everything feels normal again.

Dad's late of course. Mum makes a grand point of having to wait on the pavement. She sighs a lot and shuffles from one foot to the other, glancing at her watch but never long enough to actually check the time. I think she quite enjoys this. Like it's building on the layers of Dad being a bad guy.

"We don't have to be there right at the start," I say. "It's just a stupid high-school thing."

Mum looks away and stares down the road.

Dad finally pulls up and we climb in. Me up front, Mum in the back. Dad passes me a chocolate bar and a can.

"You OK?" he says.

"Yep."

"Excited?"

"Nope."

I glance back at Mum. She looks like she is in the doctor's waiting room, waiting to hear results of some really bad tests.

"Want some?" I say, holding out the can.

"Don't have that now," she says, shaking her head. "You'll need to pee." But I've already pulled the ring and the can is full so I have to take a few mouthfuls so it doesn't spill.

Dave waves at us from the pavement. He is getting in his van. He has his shirt and tie on again.

"Blimey," says Dad, smiling. "Where's Dave going all dressed up?" He sniggers a bit. "Not sure the trainers quite match."

I don't like the way he says that.

Mum sniffs hard and lets out a frustrated grunt. "We can't all afford new things all the time, can we? Dave is off to meet an important client."

Dad winks at me and pulls away. I lean in to the window, stare out at the world, watch the shops and houses pass by and sip the can until it's empty.

When we arrive at the high school, the car park is full and Dad has to drive out and find a space on the street. We walk in together, Dad in front, me in the middle, Mum at the back.

I don't know why they do this, this 'the three of us together' stuff. Well, I do actually. It's all Gena's fault. She came round a lot when Dad left. She came with cakes and candles and wine and she would sit with her big billowing skirts and her floaty scarves. I sat outside once, on the stairs, and listened.

"... make time for yourself..."

"... don't argue in front of James..."

"... always ensure for James's sake that you do things together. Christmas, parents' evening, that kind of thing..."

Well, Gena. You know what? It doesn't quite work like that. I'm stuck in between them, like the pull-out screen Uncle Bobby had in his hospital room. The nurse would whip it across, hiding all the things the other side shouldn't see. I'm like that screen.

"Where should we start?" asks Mum. She rests one hand on my shoulder and glances at the high-school map.

"Hey, look, James," says Dad, pointing at a poster on a wall. "They do a trip to Iceland."

"And who's going to pay for that?" mutters Mum, guiding me down the corridor. "Hardly a useful trip. I doubt James will be learning Icelandic."

It's like Mum peels off her normal self and lives in this other skin with Dad.

"Think it might be a geography trip," says Dad. "Volcanoes, glaciers, that kind of thing."

We walk along a corridor. There are loads of people. I feel tiny, like I've shrunk and I'm even smaller than normal. We go up a flight of stairs to the science bit. There are older kids demonstrating experiments. "Electrics," says Dad. "Let's have a go."

"Dave would understand all of this," says Mum. But it's so noisy Dad doesn't hear and I'm glad.

We wriggle through to a free table. There are two boys helping. One is my height and I feel better. I'm not going to be the smallest here. He shows me how to make the bulb light up. Flo is on the table next to us. Her dad is making a double-circuit thing.

"Let's find the gym," says Dad and we leave. On the way we pass the IT building. Computers line every wall.

I've never seen so many screens in one place. We stand at the door and I see Jez. He is talking to a parent about the computers. He is with two other kids. Mikey isn't there. Jez is smiling and pointing and when he looks up and sees me, he stops and he looks a bit odd, like he's not sure what he should do. He raises his hand, just a little, to wave.

"Want to go in?" says Mum but I shake my head. We turn to go but I look back at Jez and smile a bit and he smiles back.

The gym is full of different tables. There is one showing the uniform, one for bus information and then others advertising clubs and sports. It's funny seeing Mum and Dad side by side, chatting away to the teachers. Dad says something about being rubbish at science and it makes Mum smile. Maybe Gena was right. Maybe it's a good thing we are all doing this. A girl passes me a flyer about the basketball team. I take it but looking at the kids in basketball gear I'm not sure I'm going to be the school's top-scoring slam-dunker superstar. Unless the rules change and they lower the hoop. A lot.

Tomaz joins me. "The football club is over here. You coming?" I nod and follow him but I don't really want to. Jack is there, shooting the soft balls into the indoor net at the back of the gym.

Mum comes over. "James, do you remember Sanjit?"

I look at the boy with Mum and shake my head. "You and Sanjit were at music club together," says Mum. "When you were about three. Sanjit's mum and I were just remembering the show you all put on."

Sanjit's mum and dad are with him.

"You tried to balance the triangle on your ears, James, do you remember?" Um, no, Mum, I don't. "And it kept falling off and clattering to the floor!"

"And Sanjit was on the xylophone!" says Sanjit's mum. "He bashed it so hard, one of the little keys broke!"

Sanjit and I shuffle around. He puts his hand in his pocket and takes out a packet of gum.

"Want one?" he says.

Mum hates gum but I take one and say thanks. I realize Sanjit is only slightly taller than me and I really hope he is in my form.

And then a bell rings.

"That's for the head teacher's talk," says Dad, joining us. "Come on." And then he leans a little towards Mum and he lowers his voice and says, "I recognize that couple. Is that the musical-show kid? When James did the thing with the triangle?" Mum nods and they look at each other and they actually smile. Mum and Dad smile, remembering this great moment of my musical genius. OK, I'll give it to you, Gena. This is kind of working.

We follow Sanjit and his parents to the big hall. I wonder if I could balance the triangle now, on my ears.

When we've all sat down, the head teacher welcomes us all and tells us what an amazing time we are going to have.

"I need the loo," I whisper to Mum. She scowls at me and then at Dad.

"Told you that would happen," she says. "Do you know where they are?"

I nod, even though I haven't a clue. I scuttle out and a very tall man in a suit says, "Boys' toilets?" I want to say, *No I've changed my mind, I'm going home*, but I nod and he points and tells me where to go.

The toilets are a grubby cream colour and smell a bit. Someone has drawn a rude picture on the wall and then someone else has tried to wipe it off. They should have used nail polish.

I find a cubicle. The toilet is full of clogged paper. Just like India said it would be. I pee on it and then try to flush and the toilet kind of drags itself into action.

I wash my hands and go back to the hall. India is sitting with her parents. She is in between them and then on the end of the row there is an empty chair and I think of her little sister and how she should be sitting in it.

I hope India has a better toilet experience.

"You OK?" asks Dad. I nod and sit down and he taps my

knee as if to reassure me that this will all be fine. And then Mum leans in to me and mouths "You OK?" and I nod and she smiles as if to reassure me that this will all be fine.

I only went to the loo.

MUSIC

Can you balance a triangle on your ears?
Can you bash a xylophone so the key disappears?
Can you blow a trumpet so they hear it in France?
Can you play the bagpipes to make soldiers dance?
Can you unstring a harp and make a tennis racket?
Can you break a piano when you really whack it?
Can you screech a violin that makes the cats whine?
Can you drum so loud the neighbours complain every time?
I can't play a thing and I never sing a song
I hit the first note and my dog Digger is gone
My screeching sends him right out of the room
So I've given up ever trying to sing in tune.

Tuesday 26th June

Tomaz is turning out his swim bag in the car. Goggles, towel, trunks.

"You didn't bring the blue trunks," he says, shoving it all back in.

"The blue ones," says his mum, "were still in bag, soggy and smelly from last week."

"Oh," says Tomaz. "I hate the black ones. They pinch." He pulls his waistband high. "Wedgie time," he says to me and we laugh.

His mum passes back a paper bag. Tomaz pulls out two doughnuts. I take one and bite it. The jam oozes out.

"How was spelling exam?" asks Tomaz's mum.

"It was just a tiny test, Mum," says Tomaz.

She wants to know everything. What we all scored. Which words Tomaz forgot. Who got the best mark.

We turn the corner, the one with the big pub. It's a bit tricky to see because I'm on the other side but I lean forwards and check on the dinosaur. The rude words are there but this week they are smeared with bird muck, a long streak of it covering the last two letters.

"How you get that wrong?" says Tomaz's mum. "James, you get it?"

The traffic slows. I lick the jam from round my mouth. I haven't been listening.

"Which word?" I whisper to Tomaz.

"Necessary," says Tomaz. He is on his phone, flicking through the penguin game.

"No," I say. "I didn't."

The traffic crawls to a stop. We are alongside the pub car park now. It's pretty empty. Just two cars and a white van. The van has lettering down the side of it. Just like Dave's. And then I realize it is Dave's van. And then I see Dave. He is leaning against the passenger door. And then I feel really sick. And hot. My head throbs. My breath is stuck. I can't breathe.

Dave is with a lady. He has his arms round her. The lady's head is resting on his shoulder. The lady is not Mum. She has a long, blond ponytail.

"It's hard one," says Tomaz's mum. "One 'c' and two 's', I think. Yes, boys?"

Tomaz nudges me as if I need to reply.

"Um, yes," I say. I'm watching Dave stroking this

strange lady's hair.

"As hard as 'usually,'" says Tomaz's mum. "Why is there no y at front?"

Tomaz presses buttons to make the penguins leap, completely focused on the game.

The car moves on. I stretch to watch them. They are hugging again, Dave's arms wrapped tightly around the lady's body. I keep watching through the back window until the red dinosaur disappears out of sight. And then I lean forwards and stare at the car mat under my feet. The rest of the doughnut is a sticky ball in my hand.

"You OK?" says Tomaz, his fingers still madly tapping. "You're not going to be sick, are you?" He nudges the brown paper bag across the seat and elbows me. I put the doughnut inside and wipe my hands on the paper.

Dave and a woman. No new plumbing client. No late nights fixing up a company's new bathroom suite. Dave has been seeing another woman. I rub my hands hard, until the sticky mess in my palm is a mass of tiny crumbs, scattered over the car mat.

We arrive at the swimming pool car park.

"I can't believe I've got to wear these!" says Tomaz, holding up the black trunks. He seems properly irritated now. I wish I only had to worry about tight trunks.

"You stop now," says his mum.

I open the car door. They are arguing a bit in Polish so I lift the car mat and shake the doughnut crumbs on to the tarmac and then replace it.

We go into the changing rooms and I find a cubicle. I sit on the bench and lean over and hug my knees and wonder if Dave has a twin brother. But I know it's him. He had his old trainers on. The ones with the faded red stripes.

The other kids laugh, joke, their voices echoing round the changing area. Their day is normal, like mine was just ten minutes ago.

I get changed. Mum has left me a juice carton in my bag with a note on it. *From Digger, with love.* I think of Mum and how I'm going to tell her.

I follow the others out and I jump in the water and I swim the warm-up lengths as fast as I possibly can, as if my body is icy cold and I'm swimming for my life, away from everything, everyone.

I'm in bed. It's late. Mum has gone to bed. Dave isn't back. Well, of course he isn't. He's with that woman.

The orange glow from the streetlight warms my room, making familiar patterns on the wall. But there is no way I can sleep. I'm making a plan. Of how I tell Dave that I saw him. I might go for the big drama. The mighty reveal. Maybe when Sean is round. Ooh that's good. Yes, in front of Sean.

Shaggy eyebrow Dave thought his life was made. Woman, boy, dog, home, plumbing career... But the boy was no ordinary boy ... the boy saw ... the boy told ... the boy saved the day... Shaggy eyebrow Dave's life was over ... the shaggy eyebrows were done...

I hear Dave's van pull up. His footsteps slow and draggy up the garden path. His key in the lock. Mum opens the bedroom door, goes on to the landing.

"You OK, love?" she says in a whispery voice.

"Yep," he says. I can just imagine him looking up at her, all innocent. Yuck. With those stupid, shaggy eyebrows.

"You must be shattered," she says.

"Yep," he says. "But I'm fine. The night went well."

"OK, come to bed soon."

Her bedroom door clicks shut. I turn over and face the wall. *The night went well.* How dare he. Maybe I should go downstairs right now and face him. I turn back the other way. I stare at the ceiling, the orange light making shapes of fire in between the open crack of curtain.

Wednesday 27th June

It's hard today. I wanted to show Mr Froggatt my music poem but nothing feels right. Dave's a cheat. Digger still hasn't seen the special vet. All these big things. All swirling round, bumping into each other in my mind.

I go in goal at break. There's nothing else to do. Jack is on a mission to beat the Year 5 kids.

"Get back there!" he yells. "No, come forward… What you do that for?" He blames me when they score. The Year 5 kids are really good. They beat us last time. Jack hates that. One kick catches my hand and bends my fingers back. It doesn't hurt much but I say it's worse than it is. I bend over and clutch my hand and say I'm going in to find a first aider.

"You OK?" says Tomaz, walking back to take the next kick-off.

"Fine, just need ice," I say and I jog away, one hand wrapped around the other. I can't even remember which hand got caught.

India dashes over. "Oh, me and Flo saw that big kick! Is it broken? Shall I come with you?"

"No!" I say firmly. "I'm fine." And she wanders off with Flo.

I'm waiting by the office when Mr Froggatt walks past.

"You OK, James?" he asks.

"I've hurt my hand," I say. "Mrs Dawson is getting some ice." And then I can feel the tears brewing. I blink hard, try to make them stop.

"Can be quite a shock when that happens," says Mr Froggatt.

I nod. He sits down next to me. Mrs Dawson comes back with a cold pack. She looks for swelling and tests I can move my fingers OK.

"Think you'll live," she says, smiling, and she walks away.

I bend over, put my head between my knees.

"Were you in goal?" asks Mr Froggatt. I nod. "Bit tough out there, with some of that lot, I'm sure." I don't do anything, just keep my head down. "You know Yasmine in Year Five has been chosen for the county squad?" I shake my head.

The bench wobbles as Mr Froggatt stands up. He talks to a passing teacher, mutters something about meeting with him later instead. I lift my head a little. He is by the water fountain now. He comes back with a paper cup of water and sits back down. He passes me the drink and I take it.

"I could do with some help getting stuff ready for this afternoon," he says. "Just paints and paper and materials. Up for it, James?"

I nod again. The tears have gone back down. We both stand up and head to the classroom and I realize Mr Froggatt was going the other way when he saw me. He changed his plan for me. I take the ice pack off my hand and drop the paper cup in the recycling and we work quietly together, laying out the materials for the afternoon lesson.

"Think that's it," says Mr Froggatt as we put out the last paint sets. "Thanks so much, James."

"Could I show you something?" I say.

"Absolutely."

I go to my bag and get my blue book. I hand it to him and he reads the music poem quietly, smiling. And then the bell rings.

"You must keep writing, James. This is fab."

"Thanks," I say, and I look out of the window and watch everyone coming in off the field. Jack is laughing and joking, throwing the football in the air, looking back at the Year 5 kids.

Mr Froggatt looks out too. "Well, that's a relief, looks like they won. That'll make for a happier afternoon!" I laugh and he passes me the book back. "Thanks so much for sharing that with me, James."

The doors fling open. Jack is chanting, "Three–two, three–two!"

"Is your hand OK?" Tomaz says to me.

"It's fine," I say. "I'm fine."

And I really do feel so much better.

———

Dad waves from the car. He never picks me up from school. He always comes to the house. Digger is in the back. The windows are steamed up but I can see him in the boot, his pink tongue hanging out, panting. When he sees me, his ears bob up and he tries to stand but the space is too small.

"You all right, love?" says Dad.

I nod. "How come you're here?"

"Your mum and I thought it might be a bit easier today."

OK. Really strange. Something's not right. Lots of things are not right. Mum and Dad had a normal conversation. Dad's here, at school. Without Kathy.

"What's wrong?" I ask.

"Nothing," says Dad. "Jump in."

I wait for a bunch of kids to file past and then I get in.

Dad is wearing jeans.

"Haven't you been at work?"

He pulls away. "Blimey it's busy," he says, ignoring my question.

"It's a school," I say.

Dad laughs a little and pats my knee.

"What's going on?" I say. I turn and look at the back seat. Digger's bed and food are there, and my rucksack, packed for the night. And then it comes to me. Of course. Mum has found out about Dave and that lady. She's told him to leave, doesn't know how to tell me and needs tonight to get sorted. I sink down into my seat, relieved.

I won't have to tell her.

No wonder Dad looks happy and is wearing jeans. Maybe he thinks Mum might take him back. Mum and Dad might get back together! They *are* talking again... Maybe she was bagging up Dave's things and she phoned Dad, gently asking if he could pick me up straight from school.

She found out, she threw him out, the ex got his good jeans out. The story of a family reunited. Coming to a screen near you...

We pass the park and the shops.

"We'll talk in a bit, James," says Dad. "But let's get an ice cream first." He puts the radio on and turns up the volume and I see his wrist is bare. He hasn't got a watch on. He's taken off the watch Kathy gave him. This is really happening, for real.

I tap the seat in tune to the music. Dad's fingers drum the wheel. We sing the chorus.

We park in front of the ice-cream shop. Dad switches the engine off and turns to me. I look at him. He's going to tell me about Dave.

"We took Digger to the specialist vet today."

I'm very still now. I wasn't expecting any of those words.

"This isn't about Dave?" I say.

"What do you mean?" asks Dad. "Dave came with us, to see the oncologist. He's all right you know, Dave."

I clutch the seat with both hands, dig my fingernails into the leather. I was tapping them to the music just a minute ago. That feels completely bizarre now.

He thinks Dave is all right. Dad, Mum and Dave took *my* dog, Digger, to the specialist vet.

"Why didn't I know it was today?" I have to force the words out. My mouth is so dry. "I wanted to go."

"For some reason," says Dad, "they had my number as the contact. They rang first thing. There was a cancellation at the cancer vet's. I rang Mum and we all went. It was another week's wait otherwise."

"Why didn't someone come and get me?" I ask.

"You can't miss school, James, you know that. I'm sure you agree, it was best for us to take him today, at the first opportunity."

I grunt my approval.

I'm staring at the big cow on the outside of the shop. Each flavour is written on a different black patch of the cow's body. Someone's changed 'Rum and Raisin' to 'Bum and Raisin'. Cows, dinosaurs, they all get it. I'm not cross now. Just a bit scared. I turn round and look at Digger. He is panting.

"What did the cancer vet say?"

"Let's get some ice cream," says Dad, "and I'll tell you all about it. If we sit outside, Digger can come."

We get out of the car. Dad opens the boot and Digger jumps down and wraps himself around me, his tail wagging furiously.

We sit down at the little green table outside the shop. There is a water bowl for dogs and Digger slurps away.

"What flavour?" asks Dad. He looks up at the cow and reads the list. "Fancy some bum and raisin?"

I want to smile. But I point to chocolate and Dad goes inside to order. Digger sits beside me and I rub his ears.

Dad comes back with two small tubs.

"I went for bum and raisin," he says. "I'm a brave man."

I scrape the first bit of chocolate.

"I meant to say," says Dad, "Kathy wanted to come with us today but she had a stall at the wedding fair in town."

"She doesn't like ice cream," I say.

"No, I meant to the vet's."

I take a mouthful. It's got big chocolate chips.

"She doesn't like animals," I say.

"She likes Digger," says Dad.

It's annoying me that we are talking about Kathy. She's hardly important right now. "Can you just tell me about today?" I say.

"Well," says Dad, pushing his spoon into the ice cream. "Fiona was very thorough and explained everything." He puts his tub on the table. "Digger had a malignant tumour."

"I know," I say. "I found it. I've been at the appointments. He's my dog."

"OK, OK," says Dad. "Yes, he is your dog but he is also … *our* dog." He coughs a little. "Mine and your mum's." I glance at him with slanted eyes, trying not to move my head too much, sucking on the little spoon. He sounds a bit wobbly. "Fiona is very pleased with how Digger's leg is healing but she wants to make doubly, triply sure that none of the cancer is still there."

Digger lays his head on Dad's knee. Dad strokes him, over and over, the golden fur lying soft and smooth. He picks his tub up. Digger lies down, stretches out under the little table, so that he juts out on to the pavement. It makes us smile.

"She's very confident," says Dad, the words catching in his throat, "that Digger will be fine. But she wants to give him some radiotherapy."

Dad stops and swallows and stirs his ice cream. His phone beeps but he ignores it.

I lean in to Dad and tuck my head inside his shoulder. He smells good. Of Dad.

"He starts it in a week or so, once the leg has fully healed from the op. And then he'll have four treatments, each one a week apart. They put him to sleep for a short time while they zap the area. He'll have to wear a cone again to stop him licking it. Just four treatments. OK?"

I nod. Dad rests his head on mine and the three of us sit for a minute.

"Will it hurt him?" I ask and I choke a little on the spoon. It's hard to use a small spoon when you're trying not to cry. "The radio thing, will it hurt?"

"Fiona said he should be fine. He won't feel the zap and then if it bothers him after, she will give us some tablets for pain. She explained everything so clearly."

Maybe Dad could date Fiona and Mum could fall for Charlie and then Digger would really be completely cared for.

"Is it very expensive?" I ask.

"Yes," says Dad. "But it's OK."

"Lucky we've got that insurance thing."

Dad nods and picks up his ice cream and scrapes the tub.

"Want to try the last bit of bum?" he says, and I laugh

and shake my head and reach down to stroke Digger. This is all about Digger. And that's more important than anything. I don't want to think about Dave and the stupid lady. Not now.

"Let's go home," says Dad. "I want to show you something."

The traffic is heavy now and we crawl along. Digger lies down to sleep.

"I don't want Digger to have any pain," I say.

Dad glances at me and then looks back at the road.

"Everything Fiona is doing is to help him. This is a good thing, James. It just makes sure the cancer isn't there any more."

"They thought Uncle Bobby's cancer wasn't there any more."

Dad grips the wheel tight. "Bobby had a different sort of cancer," says Dad. "We can't look at this in the same way."

"How old would he be now?"

"Forty-two," says Dad. "And he'd still be my little brother."

"Wasn't much little about Uncle Bobby was there?" I say, and we both smile. "I miss him, Dad."

"I know," says Dad, and he reaches out and holds my hand and I'm very glad that horrible watch Kathy gave him is not on his wrist.

We pull up outside the house.

Kathy's car is parked on the road.

"Oh, she's home," says Dad. "I thought the wedding thing went on all day."

He sits for a moment as if he's trying to work out what to do.

"What's the problem?" I ask.

"Nothing," he says. "Nothing."

We get out and walk up the path. Digger has a long pee. He's just finishing when the door opens. Kathy is there, arms folded. She glares at Dad, her lips pressed in a thin line. Then she forces them apart.

"What the…"

Dad looks at her and raises one hand as if to put off an argument.

"I know, I know," he says. "But I thought you were working late and I wanted to surprise James."

"This is *my* house," says Kathy. "Not a bike storage facility."

Dad grabs Digger's collar to stop him running inside.

"Thanks, Kathy," he says. "Thanks for spoiling this one thing. And it may be your house but I kind of had the idea it was my home too."

Kathy grabs her keys and storms out. She brushes past

me, past Digger. He wags his tail at her. A wasted wag.

Dad lets Digger off the lead and shuts the front door. The house looks just the same to me.

"Just give me a sec, James," says Dad, and he goes to the loo and I take Digger for a drink.

I wait for Dad. I stand in Kathy's kitchen, breathing in the bleachy smell. Her kitchen is like an operating theatre again. Nothing from the party remains. But there is one difference. On the side of the fridge, held by a silver magnet, there is a leaflet from the forest. The lady with the tattoos had written down the name of the bikes we rode, in case we came again.

"James," calls Dad. "Come here."

I go into the hall and he opens the lounge door. The furniture has been pushed back against the walls to make a big space in the middle. Dad has covered the floor with an old sheet and on the sheet are three new bikes. The smallest is black with green letters and a lightning bolt on the main frame. There is a red ribbon tied round the saddle. The room smells of rubber and shiny metal. I touch the handlebars, run my hand over the seat, push down on the suspension forks. The black paint is so shiny I can nearly see my face in it.

"Wow," I say. "It's amazing."

"Well, I wanted it to be," says Dad. "I realized at the

forest how much I've missed it. Missed doing things like that with you, James."

I lean in to Dad and he puts his arm round me.

"Thanks, Dad," I say. "I love it."

"Good," says Dad.

We sit on our bikes, side by side. Dad looks over at Kathy's bike. It has a purple saddle.

"I'm sure Kathy will enjoy it," he says. He pulls the tag free so it's no longer tangled in the spokes and then he looks outside, raises his head so he can see if her car is back. "She deserves a bit of fun. Life hasn't always been easy for her. She's a good person."

"I know," I say.

"How?"

I shrug, test the breaks. "She helped me once."

Dad reaches out for me, runs his hand through my hair. "I didn't know that," he says. He's staring at me, head tilted. He wants to know more.

"Did she know you were buying the bikes?" I ask, running my hands over the gears. I want to get away from the helping thing.

"Yes, she did. She thought it was a great idea. She even said sometimes the two of us should ride our bikes and she'll walk Digger. Then we can meet up after."

I look down at the front wheel, push down on the

suspension forks. Kathy walk Digger. I can't imagine that happening.

Dad sighs. "But she didn't know they were arriving today and then I had a bit of time, after the vet's, to set them up. She's lost a few clients recently. It's making her a bit stressed."

I turn away and put my right foot on the pedal.

Dad's phone rings. It's the ringtone he uses for Kathy. "Let me just check she's OK." He goes out to the hall and talks for a minute.

I try and get both feet on the pedals but the bike tips. I wonder if I'll keep the bike at Dad's or Mum's house. And then I remember that I still have the big secret. About Dave. It comes back with a punch.

Dad rushes in, smiling. "She's parked just round the corner. She feels a bit silly for overreacting and she's coming now to see the bikes."

Digger follows Dad in. He sniffs the wheels and wags his tail and then jumps on the sofa that has been pushed back by the window. The cushions ride up and catch the windowsill. One glass sculpture wobbles and shakes from side to side. Dad dives and I jump and we both leap on to the sofa and just as Kathy's car pulls up, Dad catches it, slipping his thumb inside the glass hole. Kathy climbs out of the car. She looks over to the front window. Dad is holding the glass sculpture high in the air, as if it's worth a million pounds.

Digger is up on the sofa, his paws resting on the back and when he sees Kathy, he jumps again, excited. The other glass sculpture wobbles. I grab it fast. When I look up, Kathy has one hand covering her eyes, peeping out from underneath, her body clenched as if she's waiting for the crash. She smiles, just a tiny smile, and then drags both hands down over her face, as if she's just seen a disaster avoided. Which I suppose she has. I think it's the first time I've seen Kathy smile like that.

Thursday 28th June

Mum's friend Gena is sitting at the kitchen table. She puts down her cup of tea and smiles at me.

"You've grown, James," she says.

She always says that.

"Good day?" Mum asks.

"Yep," I say.

Digger runs in from the garden to see me. I find him a treat.

"I was just telling Gena about Digger's treatment. Your dad explained everything, yes?"

"Yep," I say and I take Digger back into the garden and throw a ball for him.

And then I wonder why Gena is here. She came a lot when Mum and Dad split up. And she came a lot when Russell texted to say he wouldn't be coming back.

Maybe Mum knows. Maybe she's found out about Dave and the lady.

Mum comes to the patio door. She's smiling.

"Sean's coming for dinner, James, OK?" I turn away and make a face and throw Digger's ball. I don't want Sean here. I never want Sean here. "Did you hear me?"

I make a noise that tells her I did.

"I've made pulled pork, your favourite."

I don't say anything. As if pulled pork makes any difference.

And then I spin round.

"Why is Sean coming, if Dave has to work?" I spit it out.

Mum stares at me, a little shocked.

"You know Dave would rather be with us."

Oh my god. My head is going to explode. Why can't she see what is happening? Digger is scrabbling in the bush for his bone so I scrabble in with him. She shouts after me.

"He starts at eight tonight so we're eating early. And then he's working Friday and Saturday. Early to late." And then she slams the patio door. I lie flat in the undergrowth, Digger's paws catching my hand as he scratches for his bone.

The doorbell rings, loud and long, and Digger pulls his head free and runs to see who it is. He has dirt all over his head and paws. He scratches at the patio door and Mum opens it. I want to go with him. I don't want Digger to be with Sean. But I absolutely do not want to go inside.

Mum glances at me and shuts the door again, but softly this time.

I kneel down into the bush and reach for Digger's bone. He's pushed it back towards the fence, in a weedy bit that escaped the clean-up. I pull it out and there, stuck to the bone, is a red strand of wool. I've not found one for ages. It's from Mum's jumper, the one she carried Digger home in when we first got him, the one that became his comfort blanket and that he chewed and ripped to pieces, red threads scattered across the entire garden. I tuck it deep into my pocket.

I can hear Dave and Sean inside. Sean's voice bangs through the house. Mum laughs. Gena calls out goodbye and then I realize she has opened the door and is saying it to me and I raise one hand. Digger runs out again. I show him the bone. He bites it hard and we play a bit of tug. I spin round and he keeps his teeth locked on, shaking it from side to side.

Sean comes out for a cigarette so I grab Digger's collar and take him upstairs, which is a bit tricky because I meet Dave on the stairs. He's got a bad foot now. Something to do with his heel. It takes him longer to go up the steps so we have to follow slowly. Digger pulls to reach Dave and wags his tail and I'm absolutely mad because Dave puts a hand back and tickles him under the chin and says, "Who's such a good dog," and all I can think about is what a horrible cheat Dave is and how I don't want him near Digger.

My room is quiet and still. Digger lies down and I give him back the bone. He's not supposed to have the bone up here but I don't care. I'm breathing hard. I'm not sure what to do. I have to tell Mum about Dave.

My poetry book is sticking out of my bag. Mr Froggatt has just caught up with the poems after he was ill. I want to see what he has written.

He's the heart of the home, my best hairy friend
I'll love him forever, to the last very end.

This is a lovely poem, James. I would love to meet Digger.

I find a pencil.

I'd like you to meet him too. He has to have radiotherapy. They make him sleep for a bit while they zap the leg.

And then I cry. I cry a lot and I try to hide it from Digger but he knows. Digger knows everything. He rests his head on my knee and I nestle into his fur.

Mum calls me for dinner. I'm hungry. I go downstairs with Digger. He lies by the table but Mum takes him and puts him in the utility room. For a second he stares through the glass and then he goes to his bed and lies down and I'm mad about that. He's got used to Dave's stupid rule. I've got to sit next to Sean while Digger has to be out of the way. I stick my fork into the bowl of pulled pork and dig out a giant piece.

"Leave some for everyone else," says Mum, smiling.

Sean gets up and takes a beer from the fridge.

"Steady, mate," says Dave. "You've had two already."

We eat in silence. Mum hums a little.

"Will you look for another job at a garage?" asks Dave. He is rubbing his head, over and over. Yeah, bet you're tired, Dave, the life you're living.

Mum leans over to me. "Sean has had to leave his job," she says. I nod. As if I'm interested. Which I'm not. "He's trying to get another one but things are tricky."

I want to say, *Everything's tricky right now, Mum,* but I don't.

I can't imagine anyone giving Sean a job. Mum suggests the local tool shop or the big homeware store.

We finish eating. The meal has raced by, as if no one really wants to be there. Mum gets yoghurts from the fridge.

"Why can't you sort me out with something, Dad?" says Sean. "I could help at this new evening thing you got going on." He laughs in a nasty way. Like a scoff. "If you can learn new skills, then it's not too late for me."

Dave glares at him.

"You know nothing about plumbing," he says. He says it in a way that sounds like he is trying to cover something up. And only I know what. Just me. I scrape at my yoghurt pot.

Sean glugs his beer and smiles at his dad, his eyes not leaving Dave's – as if he knows what Dave is really up to as well.

"Have you ever thought about college, Sean?" says Mum. "There are so many courses you could look at."

Sean's smile disappears. Dave folds his serviette over and over. Sean looks from Mum to Dave and then back again.

"Been talking, you two, have you?" says Sean. "About how I should go back to college and study some useless course?"

Mum straightens her table mat, glances at Dave.

217

"No," says Dave, very firmly. "We haven't. But you know my thoughts on that."

"Yep," says Sean. "I do. And you know mine." He sits back in his seat, kicks his feet out, taps his bottle on the table.

Mum collects the used spoons.

I get up and throw my yoghurt pot in the recycling and get Digger. He races out and rushes up to Dave and then up to Sean and he nudges Sean's elbow, which bangs the beer bottle against Sean's teeth. We all hear it. Sean jumps to his feet, slams the bottle down and then turns on Digger and raises his hand.

I yell, Mum yells and Dave leaps up.

"That was an accident!" Dave shouts. "Don't raise your hand at Digger."

Sean stares at Dave and then grabs his jacket from the back of the chair and flies out, the door slamming behind him.

The house goes very quiet. The phone rings but no one answers it.

Digger is under the table now. I join him. He is very still, a little shocked I think. I stroke him while Dave and Mum pad round the room, clearing up. They mutter about Sean and college and a car mechanic course.

"He hates talking about it," says Dave. "I thought he'd go back. He's just too proud."

"I'm sorry I mentioned it," says Mum. "I had no idea."

I can't believe Mum is actually feeling bad. As if it's her fault.

"Forget it, Jacks. And he can't be like that with Digger."

Mum stops and comes over to the table, bends down and looks at me.

"You need to leave Digger in the utility room until we've all finished in future, James," she says and then she stands back up.

So it's my fault is it?

Dave shuffles over to her and they hug.

"This is where Digger should be," I say. "Under the table."

I'm mad again. I hate Sean. I hate Dave.

"I have to go," says Dave.

Mum sniffs. She's crying, I'm sure. "At least you've got a lift tonight."

"Yep, she'll be here in a minute. She's going to pick me up on the corner."

I stare at the two pairs of feet. I say a run of bad words under my breath. And then I stand up and I shove my hands in my pockets and I face them both and I say it.

"I saw you."

Mum reaches into her apron pocket for a tissue. "What are you talking about, James?" she says, wiping her nose, her eyes.

"I saw Dave."

"What do you mean?" says Dave. He glances at Mum.

Yeah, I bet you're glancing at Mum. Worried, that's what you are, Dave.

"Outside the pub. Hugging that lady."

Dave stops and looks down. It's like he's trying to remember, trying to think. Trying to find a way out.

"What lady?" says Mum. She doesn't look the slightest bit bothered. Maybe she knows. Maybe she doesn't care. Maybe she wants rid of Dave.

"On the way to swimming," I say. "The other day. With Tomaz. We drive past that pub. You know, the one we used to go to for Sunday roast. The one with the red dinosaur."

Dave looks at Mum and she looks at him and they both sigh a bit. Why are they sighing?

"I know," I say. I'm digging my hands deep into my pockets, pushing with both fists. "I know where Dave has been all those evenings, Mum." I'm shouting a bit now. "He's not been fixing toilets or leaks."

"I know," says Mum.

"He's been with that lady…"

"I know," says Mum.

I stop. We are all quiet. Digger lifts his head from under the table.

"What do you mean, you know? How could you know?

He was hugging her, Mum. Outside a pub."

"I know," says Mum. "That was Clare, yes?"

Dave nods.

Mum sighs. She is smiling a bit.

"Why are you smiling?" I shout.

Mum rests one hand on my shoulder.

"You saw Dave's cousin, Clare. Clare's dad passed away just a few weeks ago. They've had a terrible time. Dave was comforting her. Clare helped Dave to get –" Mum stops and looks at Dave. Dave nods – "a job. She's a manager at the pub. He's been working there in the evenings to get a bit of extra money."

"Why would he do that? You can't trust him, Mum! He'll leave soon, you'll see."

Dave looks at me. His eyes scrunch as if I've sprayed them with something nasty.

"I'm not going anywhere," says Dave. "Sorry, James. But you're stuck with me."

"Then why are you not here, with Mum? Why do you need more money? You haven't before." I start to cry. I don't want to cry in front of Dave. "Why did you get the TV box if you need more money? And book bowling trips and buy drive-through burgers. All that stuff. You're lying to us!" I'm yelling it now. Digger comes out from under the table and skulks off to his bed in the utility room.

"You're a liar," I say. "Just like Russell."

Mum turns to me.

"Don't you dare," she says. "Don't you dare put Dave in the same sentence as that man and don't you dare say he's a liar."

"He doesn't need to work in the pub."

"Yes, actually," says Mum. "He does. We need the money."

"What *for?*" I yell it. Spit flies out.

Mum closes her eyes, breathes deeply.

Dave shakes his head. "No," he says.

"I'm not having this," says Mum.

"Don't, Jackie," he says.

"For *Digger*," says Mum. She says it again, very gently and very softly. "For Digger."

I stare at her and I stare at Dave. One to the other. "For Digger?" I ask.

"Yes," says Mum. She sits down. "Digger's operation and now his medicine. It's all so expensive. We were struggling to pay for the operation, let alone the radiotherapy drugs. It's thousands of pounds."

My mind races. Digger. Medicine. Cancer. Lumps. Money.

"What about the insurance?" I ask.

Dave and Mum look at each other. Dave shakes his head but Mum says, "The insurance was cancelled. Your dad cancelled the insurance. There is no insurance."

"But why?" I say. "Why would he do that?"

"Because it was expensive," says Mum.

"He thought it wasn't needed," says Dave.

"But he's got plenty of money. He's sold loads of cars. He told me. He's bought me a new bike. On that thing that's like insurance. That credit thing."

Mum looks out at the garden. Dave picks up the table mats and carries them over to the drawer.

"All that matters," says Mum, "is that Digger is getting the treatment he needs." She glances over at him in his bed, his head resting on his paws. "The three of us went to the vet's yesterday and we've worked it all out."

"I don't believe any of it," I shout. "You're just telling me all this to try and blame Dad for everything. Dad wouldn't do that. He wouldn't."

I grab the phone and run out of the room and up the stairs. Mum calls after me. Dave calls my name too. But I'm not going back. As if I would. I slam my bedroom door and dive on to my bed.

I'm breathing really hard. I tap buttons on the phone and find 'Peter J'. It rings and rings and rings and then Dad's answerphone kicks in and his voice is all perky and car salesy. He says he has lots of 'great new bargains'. I throw the phone and it bounces off the wall and the batteries come out and roll away. I open my drawer and get out the emergency brick mobile phone. It's out of charge. Completely dead.

I'm seething. Every bit of me is mad.

I want to get Digger but I don't want to go back downstairs. I hear Mum call out to me again but I get under the duvet and wrap it tight around me, pulling the corners in, my breath fast and angry, my head pounding, the words they said banging around in my mind.

After a while, Dave comes up. I know it's him. He struggles on the stairs with his bad foot. He knocks on the door, a gentle tap. He waits. I bury my head deeper.

"James, I'd like to talk to you." He knocks again. "I'd rather not speak through the door."

We wait, both of us. And then my swimming medals clink. They hang on hooks on the back of the door. He comes in and sits on the bed. I don't want him on the bed. I squirm further into the corner.

"Are you OK?" he says.

I want him to go. I don't want him sitting here, trying to take over everything. Mum, Dad, Digger. I hate him. I hate him.

"Your dad and I had a chat, James. The other day. Everything is fine. He didn't think Digger would ever need the insurance and, at the time, he needed the cash and the insurance was expensive."

"I don't believe you." Every word is like stone. Heavy and

grey and hard to move out of my mouth.

How dare he talk to my dad. About my dog. Our dog.

"OK, well, I'm going to finish talking and then you can decide either way."

I squeeze my lips very tight.

"I can understand," he says, "what your dad did."

I'm getting really hot. I lift the duvet slightly. I can just see him. He folds his arms. He stares at the floor while he talks.

"I really can. I've been there. Money is tight and certain things have to go. A lot of people don't even insure their pets in the first place."

I force my lips apart. "He wouldn't do that." Every word is hard to say. "He bought me a bike."

Dave rocks his legs a little, rubs his head. "And that's a great thing. He's your dad. And you know what, James? He's started the insurance again. Digger is covered now for anything else that pops up."

"But not for the cancer."

"No. Not for that," he says, and he leans down to pick up one of the phone batteries from the floor. "But we're sorting that. And your dad is helping too."

"Why didn't you tell me you were working at the pub? Why did you lie?"

"I couldn't get extra plumbing hours. Business has been

quiet recently. And I didn't want you to know it was for Digger. I didn't want you to know…"

He picks some fluff from his shorts, refolds his arms.

"What Dad had done," I say.

We are quiet for a moment. I shove my pillow against my eyes. Wipe them a bit.

"I suppose so, yes," says Dave. "Your dad's a good bloke. But he should have talked to us before cancelling it."

"To Mum," I say. "He should have talked to Mum."

Dave stands up. "Yes," he says. "He should have talked to your mum."

He picks up the other battery and the phone that I threw. He fixes it back together, clicking the plastic in place. And then he puts it on my bedside table. He's limping on that bad foot. Mum keeps telling him to get better trainers. And then I start to cry. I think of Dave in his horrid old trainers with his painful heel and I think of him working all day and then going to the pub and working all night. For Digger.

I bury my face in the pillow.

I want to say something.

I want to say thank you.

But I can't.

Nothing will come.

Dave rests his hand on the duvet and pats my shoulder. Very gently. As if doing it through the duvet might be OK.

And then he opens the door and leaves and closes it quietly behind him, the medals clinking very slightly. And I wish he had stayed just a little bit longer.

ONE WEEK LATER

Friday 6th July

Digger is at my feet, asleep.

"He's doing OK," says Dave.

"Yep," I say.

"Not had any painkillers yet," says Dave.

"Nope," I say. I rub the area near to where they zapped.

Digger lifts his head, nuzzles in, scrapes at the cone. I feel bad for disturbing him.

"Sounds like a fancy animal hospital, that," says Dave. He rubs Digger's head. "You deserve it though, mate, don't you?"

"We had to go all the way to Liverpool," I say. "They had game consoles in the waiting room."

"Wow, pets have really come on," says Dave. "They'll be emailing next."

I smile and rub Digger's chin where he likes it.

"Were school OK about you not being there in the afternoon?"

"Yeah, Mr Froggatt's the best."

Dave nods. "Your dad coming soon?" he says.

"Yep."

Dave has his Friday night beer and his comfy sweatpants on. "Taking the mutt?" he says, stroking Digger. "Hey, Digs, you off again?"

"Yep," I say. Dave calls him Digs and no one else ever has and I don't mind.

I don't mind much these days about Dave.

The football is about to start.

"It's a big game, yeah?" I say.

Dave looks at me and slaps one hand over his face. "'Big' is a slight understatement!" he says.

I fiddle with Digger's cone, check it's not too tight.

Dave swigs his beer. "You back Sunday?" he says.

"Yeah."

"That's good," says Dave.

I hear Dad's car pull up outside. I always know it's his car. He has this thing when he swings up to the house, like the car doesn't really slow down. It just arrives.

"Dave," I say.

"Blimey," says Dave, leaning forwards, staring at the screen. "Why's he done that?"

"What?" I ask.

"Changed the starting line-up."

"Oh," I say. "I don't know."

"Madness," says Dave. "Sorry, mate, were you going to ask me something?"

I don't mind when he calls me mate now.

"Just wondered if maybe we could do that bowling trip on Sunday night, or next week or something, you know."

Dave looks up at me and taps his beer and strokes Digger and he says, "Love to, mate." The words stumble a bit. "I'll get it booked."

I nod and grab Digger's collar. He stretches to his feet, looks up at me with his huge brown eyes.

"Thanks," I say, and I quickly glance at Dave.

He nods and then he says, "Have a great weekend."

Mum is in the hall, looking out of the window. "Your dad's here," she says.

I get my bag and Digger's things and give her a hug. "See you Sunday, Mum," I say.

"Yes, love," she says.

I go down the path. Digger pulls when he sees Dad climb out of the car. He is in his work clothes still, his tie pulled low.

"Hey, James," he says. He hugs me and takes my bag and we lift the boot.

Digger jumps up, with us both supporting his bad leg, even if he doesn't need it. Dad clips Digger in. He has to make the strap longer because the cone is in the way.

"How's he doing?"

"Good," I say. I go to the back door. But then I see Kathy isn't with Dad so I get in the front seat. And then I'm a bit surprised because right there, on the dashboard, is my present and card that I had tried to give Dad the night of the birthday party. The paper is ripped a little.

Dad climbs in. It's raining now and he wipes the drops off his shirt, rolls his sleeves up. He has Uncle Bobby's watch on again.

He takes the present and puts it on his lap. "I am so sorry, James."

I don't know what to say, so I ask, "Where's Kathy?"

"Kathy and I had a bit of a … disagreement. It's just you and me this weekend."

"Oh," I say. I stare out of the window. It feels really odd. Last time I saw Kathy was with the bikes and she'd been OK after. "Has she gone away?"

"Yes," says Dad. "Just for the weekend, to see her folks. She wanted a bit of time on her own."

It's odd but I'm not sure I like the news.

"Is it because I'm coming?"

Dad spins round fast and says, "No, absolutely not. This is about me and Kathy. We just need to work a few things out. She said to say hi and give Digger a pat. It will be fine, I'm sure."

I wonder if Kathy has asked for a ring, like the people at

the party said she wanted.

Dad smooths the wrapping paper, tries to tidy up the ripped corner. "We were doing a bit of cleaning and sorting and I found this under the bed."

I wonder if they found the blue nail polish too.

"Can I open it now?" he says.

"If you want."

He starts to break the Sellotape. It's not hard. It's all a bit bashed up.

There is a knock on the window. It's Mum. It's pouring down. She still has her apron on. She points to the pocket.

"I need to give you this for Digger," she says.

Dad yells, "Get in!"

She dives on to the back seat and there we are. Mum, Dad, Digger and me. All in the car with the rain pouring down.

"It's his painkillers," she says. "I forgot to put them in his bag because he hasn't needed them. But just in case. Fiona said only to use them if we think he's uncomfortable."

Digger's head is over the back seat, the cone bent a little to make it possible. He licks Mum's cheek and she tickles him under the chin.

The wrapping paper is off. Dad turns the present over. We are all quiet. Just the rain, tapping on the windows.

It's a photo. From the day we brought Digger home.

He is a tiny puppy, nestled in Mum's arms. The photo is mainly of Digger, but Dad's cheek is just showing and my hand is there too, stroking Digger's head. Mum has the red jumper on that became Digger's comfort blanket, the one he chewed into a thousand threads.

Dad holds the photo up so Mum can see it clearly. No one says a thing. It's the four of us in the photo and the four of us in this car with the rain pounding down and I think we all know that in some way, whatever happens, some things in life will always be about the four of us.

Mum pats my shoulder and then she pats Dad's shoulder and she climbs out. It's still raining but she walks slowly back up to the house.

"It's very special, James. Thank you," says Dad. "And I'm so sorry I didn't open it on the night." He wraps the paper back round it to protect it and puts it on the back seat.

"Can we get take out?" I say.

"Let's pick up Chinese on the way home," says Dad. The word *home* hangs in the air.

"Sounds good," I say.

He pulls away, like Dad always does, with the tyres squealing on the wet road.

TWO WEEKS LATER
Friday 20th July

Mr Froggatt has blown up balloons and left party poppers on our desks. There is a spread of snacks. Crisps and sausages and biscuits. Lots of us have brought gifts for him. Wine, chocolates, boxes of treats.

The whiteboard is covered in a giant poem. Mr Froggatt has written the first four lines.

> Our last day together, it's been quite a blast,
> But today you're off to high school at last!
> I'll miss you, it's been fun, you're such a great bunch,
> Try to finish these lines before your party lunch!

There are lots of lines with gaps for us to fill in. Tomaz chooses the first one.

> How do you feel on the last day of school?
> Horrified, excited, tearful or _____

He picks up the red marker pen and writes 'cool'. I give him a thumbs up.

Raj chooses a line near the end.

From our seven weeks together, go through your memories to find
    What's that? _____ sticks in my mind.

Raj fills in the gap.

What's that? <u>Mr Froggatt's bow tie</u> sticks in my mind.

India is waiting for the pen. She's chosen her line.

            What will you do when school is out?
    Cry, party, scream or _____

Margo elbows her and says 'shout'. But India isn't listening. She's got the pen and she's started writing. The words climb up the side of the board in a spidery trail.

    Cry, party, scream or <u>feel really really sad because</u>
    I won't see my friends all summer because I
    am going to France for four weeks and I'll miss
    everyone and Ginger has to go into a cattery.

She runs out of space and Flo wants the pen. She has to reach high to fill in the gap.

> There's one thing I'll miss about this amazing place
> It's the fact I won't _____

Flo sniffs quite hard and lifts the pen.

It's the fact I won't *see my best friend's face*.

India wraps herself around her and then Margo and Eva and Freya join in until they are one small huddle.

Flo turns back to the board and adds an *s* to *face*.

I find a line I like. I think Mr Froggatt might have written it for me.

> You're all growing up, nearly teenagers, go figure!
> This summer I'm most excited _____

I finish it easily.

This summer I'm most excited *to spend time with Digger*.

We spend the rest of the morning talking and laughing and watching cartoons while Mr Froggatt opens his cards and presents. Eva passes Mr Froggatt a giant gift bag.

"Hope you like it!" she says. "It's from everyone. We all chipped in!"

He pulls out a bright red onesie with a Manchester United logo.

"Onesie, onesie, come to me, come to me!" he says, and he hugs it tight and then puts it on, over his shirt and trousers. "I don't think I shall ever take it off! Thanks so much."

We are joking around and in the chaos of it all I watch Philip go round to the back of Mr Froggatt's desk and leave a piece of paper, folded in two.

The head teacher comes in and talks to us about how brilliant we've been, which isn't really true. She tells a few funny stories about things we've done over the years and passes us each a photo of us on the first day of school in Reception and one of us taken yesterday. They are on the same piece of card and she has written a good luck message at the bottom.

"We'll do the farewell properly at the end-of-day assembly," she says. "But I wanted you to have the photos now, so you can enjoy them with your friends." She turns to Mr Froggatt. "I've managed to persuade Mr Froggatt to stay on and teach Year Six next year." We all cheer. I'm a bit jealous. They get a whole year of him.

"But I'll only agree to stay on," says Mr Froggatt, "if I can wear my onesie every day." She laughs and leaves and Mr Froggatt goes behind his desk and sits down in his chair.

We look at our photographs. In the Reception one, I'm sitting cross-legged on the floor in between Raj and Philip. My right knee has a giant plaster on it. I'd fallen off my bike a few days before and taken the skin right off. Everyone has their arms folded. Apart from Philip – he's pulling on his shoe's Velcro strap.

"We look SO young!" shrieks Freya. "Look, there's the twins! That was just before they moved to Australia."

"Wish I was in it," says Flo, staring at the photo. She joined in Year 3.

"My bottom teeth are missing!" shouts Margo. She elbows Freya. "Do you remember? I lost them *really* early, before anyone else?"

"Look at my fringe!" says Eva. "What was my mum thinking?"

"My hair looks well sharp," says Jack.

"Shame you didn't have your onesie yesterday for the photo, Mr Froggatt!" says Raj, and we all look over at him but he isn't listening. He has opened Philip's piece of paper. He is staring at it. He looks up, searches for Philip, asks him to come over. They chat for a bit. Mr Froggatt claps his hands and stands up and clears his throat.

"I've just been given the most amazing gift. We have a real talent in the room. Philip has agreed I can share this." He holds up the piece of paper. It is a pencil sketch of Mr Froggatt. He is leaning on his desk, legs outstretched but crossed at the ankles, holding the red poetry box. He is smiling and looking out at the room. It is so good that we all gather round his desk, staring at the drawing.

"It looks exactly like you," says Tomaz.

"That's the way you smile," says Raj. "The upper lip bit. It's brilliant."

Philip shrugs and picks at his nails.

"Thank you, Philip," says Mr Froggatt. "I'll treasure it and I'll look forward to hearing about your future success. The high school has a superb art department." Philip nods as if he knows.

The bell rings. Everyone races out. The lunch staff have put on a special spread for our last day. Burgers and chips with fizzy drinks. Mr Froggatt folds his onesie, puts his gifts carefully away to take home. I hover next to his desk.

"Hey, James," he says. "Are you OK?"

I nod. He looks up to check the others are on their way out. "I'm glad you've stayed behind. I wanted to ask you how Digger is."

"He's good," I say. "He's there right now, having his third treatment. Mum's taken him. With Dave. Just one more to go after this."

"That's great news," says Mr Froggatt. "What a dog!"

He lifts up the poetry box.

"I've got five books to look at over lunch break. My last job. Is yours in there?"

"Yeah," I say. "But not to share."

"I can't wait to read it," says Mr Froggatt.

I feel in my pocket for the piece of paper.

"I wrote something different last night. My book was downstairs and I wrote it late so it's on paper. I wanted to show you." I pull the paper out and unfold it. The red thread of wool that I found in the garden is stuck on the page, underlining the title. For a second I'm worried the first line doesn't sound quite right. But I pass it over. He starts to read out loud.

THE RED THREAD
I was down on my knees in the garden at home

India and Flo burst into the room. Mr Froggatt stops. They are searching for something, India's jumper I think. They turn out the lost property box. Mr Froggatt carries on, reading in his head. When he is finished, he neatly folds the paper and passes it back to me.

"James," he says and then he sniffs and sits back on his desk and stares at the floor. "That is amazing. You must promise me you will carry on writing." I put the poem back in my pocket and nod, gently.

"Thanks," I say and I look at him and he knows I don't just mean about words on a piece of paper.

"You've got to stop that, Jacks," says Dave, smiling. Mum's bought another little dish of sausages in for Digger. "He'll get fat."

"I don't care," says Mum. "He can have whatever he wants. Three treatments down, one to go. We're getting there, hey, Digger?"

We both stroke him and glance at the TV. Dave is flicking through the channels. He finds the football and me and Mum yell, "No!" He shrugs and smiles and his shaggy eyebrows lift a little.

Digger gets to his feet and walks into the kitchen.

"He's thirsty," says Mum.

"All those sausages," says Dave.

I go with Digger to his bowl to make sure he can drink OK with the cone on.

He drinks and goes outside and I watch him from the window.

My school bag is right there and I remember Mr Froggatt had returned my poem. He passed it to me at the end of the day with a quiet nudge and a hand on my shoulder.

"Glad you went back and did that one," he had said and I nodded.

AN IMPORTANT PERSON

You can get it wrong.
You can be mistaken all along.
Shaggy eyebrows, honest and true
Working long hours to get us all through
Trying his hardest to make it all pay
To do the right thing at the end of the day
I didn't realize I live with someone true and brave
He's not my dad, but he's my friend and his name is Dave.

I like the sound of Dave. Can he wiggle his shaggy eyebrows?
Or knit them into interesting shapes?

I laugh, very loud.

Dave comes in and opens the fridge. "What's so funny, mate?" he says.

"Nothing, Dave," I say. "Nothing." And I join Digger in the garden and kick the ball and throw it against the panel that makes the banging noise. It bangs. And I'm glad. Everything is normal.

THE RED THREAD

I was down on my knees in the garden at home
Trying to help Digger find his new bone
He'd pushed it way back and I found this instead,
from the jumper he chewed, one single red thread.
I've not found one for ages, it was like saving a winner
With Uncle Bobby yelling, "Six more before dinner!"
One single red thread, the only one left to find,
One single red thread, thoughts race through my mind
Of the jumper he chewed until ragged and torn
A comfort as a puppy, when eight weeks newborn.
One single red thread, and it's how I feel about Digger
The thread that runs through us and makes our love bigger.

Acknowledgements

Over the last six years, my wonderful agent, Gill McLay, has been my sole reader and for that I send a huge thank you for your belief in me and your encouragement and guidance. Ruth Bennett, Ella Whiddett and the team at Stripes, you have made this journey a joy – many thanks. Thy – the cover is perfect, thank you.

To my dear family, fruits and friends – thank you for your faith in me and I hope you find happy recompense in Digger! Mum – you gave me a love of words and of the ridiculous and it pains me you cannot share this ride. I hope you know. Nick and our precious sons – thanks for teaching me so much about life and for believing this day would happen. Fiona – thanks SO much. And lastly – to our gorgeous Bernese mountain dog Texi, taken from us far too early – without her, this book would not exist.

About the author

Ros Roberts grew up when phones were attached to the wall by wiggly wires and music was taped on to cassettes. Amazing teachers encouraged her love of writing, setting her daily challenges to create poems to read to the class. She became a teacher herself; in her own classroom, free writing was a daily necessity and she felt privileged to watch the children's progress when words flowed without boundaries. Ros loves the rain (at all times, anytime), eating brunch, playing tennis and watching TV. She loves dogs too – her family's heartbreak when they lost Texi, their beautiful Bernese mountain dog, inspired her debut children's book *Digger and Me*.

Ros and her family have enjoyed living abroad in Vancouver, B.C. and Austin, Texas, but she is very happy and proud to be back living with her husband and three sons in the north of England, where her roots lie.

@rosiroberts   @rosrobertswriter

Why not try one of Mr Froggatt's poetry prompts yourself?
There's only one rule: have fun!

What sort of creature would you be?
Giraffe, spider, pig or flea?
Here's mine, I hope you defo agree!
That an eight-legged octopus would look great as me!

OCTOPUS

I'd live in a cave among a forest of kelp
I'd be alone and would need no one to help
Me – catch my prey and swim and dive
Crab, shrimp, fish to keep me alive
Squirting ink at any chasing shark
Darting deep to escape in the dark
Of my cave where I'd live with my three beating hearts
Three! Imagine how much love I could impart
but I'm a solitary soul, with nine brains for good measure
I'm the genius of the seabed, I'm a creature to treasure.

**Turn the page to see what James and his
classmates came up with…**

I'd be a Bocian
A big white stork
They have a nest on my
Babcia's house
On a platform.
They come for the summer
And fly to afrika for the
winter.
I would love that.
~~My bab~~
I love them. My Babcia and
the storks.
I see them every summer
when we go to Poland.

by Tomaz

A sloth living up in the trees in the zoo
Safe in a zoo - no prediturs to get you
Sleep all day
Hang and sway
Come down onse a week for a poo.

by Raj

If my days as a human were truly gone
I'd come back as a beautiful, graceful swan.
White as snow, over the lake I'd glide
With a cygnet paddling along beside.

by Margo

Bingo!
A flamingo
Pink all over and long ~~spindlee~~ spindly legs
But I ~~HATE HATE HATE~~ shrimp – it makes me feel sick!
So I'm hopeing strawbery ice-cream would do the trick
Would that turn me pink? I think so of corse
A flamingo I'd be, or if not a horse
Or a cat,
So I could play with Ginger
Hows that?

by India

Polar bear, polar bear every time
Majestic, massive, mindful
Prowling over the glacier

D
i
v
i
n
g

for a seal
Building a den for my cubs in the winter
To ‑EMERGE‑
On the glistening snow of spring.

by Eva

I would be a ginee pig
Chessnut brown
So I could live in the hutch
And nibble dandilions.

by Flo

TIGER

No one would ~~bor~~ bother me
I could ~~bite~~ eat them if they
did

by Philip

A ~~Cheater~~ cheetah with sharp spots
Farstest on the planet
but not in the ~~see~~ sea.

by Jack

Camel with a hump
Or an elephant with a trunk
Or a giraffe with a neck stretched tall
Or – oh I don't really know at all
I quite like being just as I am
I'll stay Freya the girl – I'm a big fan!

by Freya

A dolphin would be the best
Swim with your friends, on the
crest of a wave,
~~Chase all the boats~~
Chase shoals of fish, follow the
boats sailing by,
Dive into the sea
and ~~dissapear~~ disappear
until up you leap, under a ~~pink~~ sunset sky!

by James